The Last Hunt

Jackson S. Whitman

Order this book online at www.trafford.com
or email orders@trafford.com

Most Trafford titles are also available at major online book retailers.

© Copyright 2017 Jackson S. Whitman.
All rights reserved. No part of this publication may be reproduced, stored in a retrieval system, or transmitted, in any form or by any means, electronic, mechanical, photocopying, recording, or otherwise, without the written prior permission of the author.

Print information available on the last page.

ISBN: 978-1-4907-8074-0 (sc)
ISBN: 978-1-4907-8076-4 (hc)
ISBN: 978-1-4907-8075-7 (e)

Library of Congress Control Number: 2017901692

Because of the dynamic nature of the Internet, any web addresses or links contained in this book may have changed since publication and may no longer be valid. The views expressed in this work are solely those of the author and do not necessarily reflect the views of the publisher, and the publisher hereby disclaims any responsibility for them.

Any people depicted in stock imagery provided by Thinkstock are models, and such images are being used for illustrative purposes only.
Certain stock imagery © Thinkstock.

Trafford rev. 02/10/2017

www.trafford.com

North America & international
toll-free: 1 888 232 4444 (USA & Canada)
fax: 812 355 4082

DISCLAIMER

This is a work of fiction. "Names, characters, and incidents used herein are simply the product of my imagination. Any resemblance to actual persons, living or dead, is entirely coincidental."... If you believe that, I've got a bridge that I'll sell you, cheap. I see this disclaimer, or something similar, on most works of fiction. The two statements, in and of themselves, are, in most cases, fiction as well. As an author, I use life experiences for all the characters and events depicted. To deny this is ludicrous. I've been around hunters and bush pilots most of my life. While I've obviously changed the names and usually melded various personalities into the story, the characters depicted herein are based on my experiences with a multitude of the finest people on earth.

CENTRAL ARKANSAS LIBRARY SYSTEM
ADOLPHINE FLETCHER TERRY BRANCH
LITTLE ROCK, ARKANSAS

ACKNOWLEDGEMENTS

Several good friends deserve a word of thanks for providing editorial comments, encouragement, and in some cases, whiskey. To Ken and Barb Deardorff, Mary and Jim Odden, Larry Kaniut, the late Harry Chartier, the late Ralph Salvas, and Emily and LeRoy Whitman, my gratitude. Too, many thanks are extended to the many bush pilots throughout Alaska with whom I spent thousands of hours flying, especially Harley McMahan, Ken Lewis, and Rick Swisher.

Finally, my wife Lisa is responsible for the book becoming a reality. The manuscript, unpolished, sat around for many years until Miss Lisa took it upon herself to edit out the bad and get it published. I simply spun a story; she did all the work. To her, a heartfelt MWAH!

I
GETTING STARTED

The roar from the gun was deafening, even with the ear protectors. The punishment meted out, however, was only to my shoulder. Downrange, the third small hole that instantaneously appeared in the paper touched the previous two holes, and all were just a tad high, within an inch of the center ring.

"Enough paper shooting for me," I said. "God wouldn't have put blood into a critter if he hadn't intended 'em to bleed. This rifle is ready to go." With the task of sighting in the guns completed, we were on our way.

Gus and I had been planning for two weeks. For us, that was a long time. The usual trip, whether it was for hunting, fishing, or trapping, was planned with nothing more than a short phone call the night before. We had been on some foolhardy outings before, but for two over-the-hill sheep hunters, this one was big.

In years past, we had chased after with gun, rod, trap, or snare nearly every species of animal that Alaska had to offer. All outings were successful; a good percentage even netted meat for the freezer or furs to be sold. Success shouldn't be measured by the size of the trophy, but by the good times and memories that the trip produced.

Born of a deep respect for the animals and the land, Gus and I had developed a kinship that had lasted solidly for the past two decades.

My forty-seven years made me the youngster on the trip. Gus never called me Charlie, but rather, "the Kid"; but he himself would never fess up to an actual age. If I had to guess, I would have said sixty when I saw him in his behind-the-desk, oil executive role during most of the year. A vastly different guess would have been warranted when I was with him in the mountains. He was transposed from a serious and efficient administrator to a twenty-five-year-old happy-go-lucky hellion, full of practical jokes, wry humor, and an ever-present Copenhagen bulge in his lip. Most trips on which we spent more than three or four nights, Gus would develop a brown stain on his graying whiskers from the tobacco spittle that he never quite figured out how to eject fully past his chin. Actually, he was probably no more than ten years my senior. I would never know.

Twenty or twenty-five years old was probably a safe age for Dall sheep hunters. Much past that, and most of us aren't willing to bust our asses to get "just one more drainage over" to find that forty-inch ram. Gus and I had each taken four rams; and those sheep hunts, whether we punched our tags or not, had always been the ones most talked about over the frequent poker games, campfires, or midnight drives to the nearest salmon stream. Because all sheep hunts entailed long packs over pretty serious terrain, neither of us ever brought along a camera. It was regarded as a two-pound luxury, and when every ounce was critical, we always opted for a plastic flask of Wild Turkey in its place. That way, Gus always argued, we could vividly describe the glacier-covered mountains, the snow-covered tents, and the awesome size of the rams; and nobody could dispute our claims. With pictures, it was easier for someone to point out all the bullshit we were shoveling out.

It was morning of the eleventh of September. A few fall days had hit the Anchorage bowl, but the Chugach Range above town had an inviting skiff of "termination dust" coating the upper three thousand feet. We knew we were pushing the weather, but Gus and I'd both had professional commitments that we had somehow let interfere with our hunting season. My minerals exploration business kept me and several employees busy during the short field season of Alaska's summers.

We were finally loaded up and on the road in Gus's big Ford. A Subaru wagon went scooting past us on the Glenn Highway, and Gus made some profane remark about the truthfulness of the guy's bumper sticker: "Happiness Is Anchorage in the Rearview Mirror." Gus claimed he disliked bumper stickers but, nonetheless, had a couple of his own. One was actually a National Rifle Association membership sticker, the other a bona fide bumper sticker that his wife had covertly plastered there in response to another hunting season she spent alone: "Nuke the Unborn Gay Whales."

We had made arrangements with Mica Meyers, a well-known sourdough and hunting guide, to provide us with air transportation to a remote area near the head of the Matanuska Glacier in the Chugach Mountains. Gus and I had flown with him on many previous hunting trips and were more than comfortable with his knowledge of his planes and the country. Gus always referred to Mica as Mr. Time, not because of his seeming ability to never age, but because of his ability to always be a day or two late picking us up. Gus always remarked that he always showed up in the nick of time, just before the last of the freeze-dried food was forcing us toward suicide.

Three hours later, and still an hour early, we pulled in to the Myers' driveway. Gus was expounding on the certain desirability of Mica's twenty-five-year-old daughter, when he suddenly jerked the pickup off the dirt road and into the pea-gravel borrow pit. An abrupt stop was punctuated with an even more abrupt expletive, as the high-pitched roar of a SuperCub drowned out the string of adjectives flowing from Gus's spit-stained lips. The Cub had lifted off the driveway no more than thirty yards in front of us, and the oversized tundra tires of the plane had missed us by less than the antler spread of a yearling bull moose.

I reminded Gus that the hand-painted "Caution—Aircraft" sign was not to be taken lightly, as Mr. Time's driveway was also his landing strip under certain wind conditions. Gus's only reaction was to step out of the truck then drop his red long handles to moon the airplane as it circled back over us to see if we were still alive. Gus drove the remaining four hundred yards in the borrow pit, reluctant to chance another encounter with a propeller.

We were met at the house by a scruffy black mutt who bore a slight resemblance to a shepherd. He stood up and emitted a hoarse bark but seemed to be looking several degrees to our left. He hobbled down off the porch, limped over to an equally scruffy black spruce, and slowly grabbed a branch in his mouth. He shook the branch a few times, and getting no response, he plopped back down. I knocked on the door; and the black mutt staggered to his three feet, gummed the spruce a few more times, and drooped his head. No response came from within the house. Scruffy headed back for the porch, bumped smack-dab into Gus, raised his leg, and pissed on Gus's boot, before he stumbled back up the stairs. I pointed out that the dog had more excuse than some people who treated Gus with as much respect. The old cur's eyes were the color of milk; he had one foot missing, probably lost to one of Mica's traps; and the fleshy end of his nose was a jumbled mass of wet scar tissue. That old boy could probably attest to the rigors of bush life better than most of this country's so-called sourdoughs. Being blind in one eye and not able to see out of the other, the dog had probably mistaken Gus for the spruce. The puddle of piss that Gus was standing in wasn't meant as a gesture of disrespect.

Over the next two hours while we awaited Mica's return, Gus and I wandered around the several outbuildings Mica had accumulated over the past half century. A screened meat shed held several moose and caribou quarters, hung in neat rows and enveloped in individual cotton meat sacks. The strong smell of black pepper hung in the air, an often-used method to repel blowflies from aging meat.

The airplane hangar door was open, and parts of at least twenty different planes littered the surroundings. A Federal Aviation Administration certificate proclaiming that Mr. Mica M. Meyers had twenty thousand hours of logged flight time was thumbtacked above the workbench. It attested to the fact that all the wrecked aircraft were probably salvaged by Mica, not caused by him. The date on the certificate was 1971. Gus and I wondered just how many hours old Mr. Time had accumulated in the intervening fifteen years.

On the hangar wall next to the FAA certificate was an old black chalkboard. A neatly hand-printed table listed departure dates, number of people, drop-off location, and pick-up dates and times of about eight hunting parties that Mica had out. Since few of the air taxi operators in Alaska outfitted all their planes with radio equipment, it seemed like a good system for keeping track of all the clients and was, in effect, an informal flight plan should anything go wrong.

Charlie Lander/Gus Harms, 9/11/86-noon, Futility Landing Strip, and 9/21/86-noon were all neatly printed as the bottom entry. All departure and pick-up times were listed as noon. This was Mica's way of saying he'd be there when he got there, and noon was easy to write.

"Futility Landing Strip" was our listed destination. For some reason that didn't sound overly inviting. Gus insisted, however, that Mica's spelling was probably not too good; he thought it was called Fertility Strip. Gus had a humorous way of squashing any remnants of doubt I had.

Mica pulled the mixture knob stopping the prop, and the Cub coasted to a stop alongside the plywood hangar. He dropped the airplane's door and backed out of the small cockpit, hopping to the ground. With a broad grin and a boisterous howdy, he climbed the pole ladder, retrieved the gas hose, and hopped up on the plane's grossly oversized, mushy tire. He inserted the nozzle in the wing tank and spryly hopped back to the ground. As he walked over, the old black mutt limped toward us too; and at the sound of Mica's voice, I could almost see a wag of the scraggly tail.

"Ol' Smokey's looking pretty tired!" Gus shouted.

"If you'd been chewed on by a grizz, frostbit on the face, spent three nights in a wolf trap at 50 below, and not had any female companionship for three years, I 'spect you'd be a bit testy too!" Mica hollered back.

I would have bet a month's wages on what Gus would say next. He always said it.

"Hello, Mr. Meyers. By god, you're just in time. I figured the full moon I flashed you a couple hours ago would keep you flying for the next three days!"

Mica laughed as we all shook hands and went through the "how are ya" formalities. We immediately got down to the business at hand.

Gus asked Mica about the sheep populations and the weather forecasts. As we helped transfer more moose quarters from the back of the Cub to the meat shed, Mica filled us in on the particulars.

"You boys know the weather could change anytime, and chances of tipping over a sheep are a bit lower'n poor should a storm hit. Findin' a white critter in a snowstorm's harder'n findin' a virgin in a whorehouse," Mica yelled. Mica always yelled. Twenty thousand hours in a small airplane doesn't result in acute hearing.

According to Mica, Flight Service was predicting that the big low pressure moving in from the Gulf of Alaska would boil over the Chugach Range and into the Copper River Basin by late afternoon. They were forecasting winds aloft that would produce some moderate to severe turbulence, and some snow was expected above three thousand feet. As far as I was concerned, that wasn't necessarily bad news. Flight Service was almost always wrong, so chances are it would be good weather for a while. "Katie, bar the door" when they predicted clear skies and unlimited visibility. Tie down the planes and get ready for a storm.

The aviation gas was splashing into an ever-widening puddle behind the right wing of the Cub when we returned from the meat shed. Mica calmly climbed up on the landing gear, pulled the hose from the wing, and walked around the front of the plane to reinsert the nozzle in the other wing tank. After a few minutes, the second tank was full; but instead of putting our gear in the Cub, Mica yelled that we should pull the truck over to old Delta. From previous trips we'd taken with him, Gus and I knew that

Mica named his aircraft based on the last letter in the plane's identification number. Gus and I glanced over the assortment of planes Mica had lined up opposite the hangar and found an old Cessna 180, number N2065D.

While we transferred the backpacks and rifles from the truck to the airplane, Mica and Smokey teamed up to piss in the puddle of spilled avgas. This certainly seemed a bit odd. "What the hell you doin', Mica?" I shouted while Gus stared openmouthed.

"When I was just a pup in this business, I found one day that I was in dire need of some 80-87 avgas. I'd used up all the storage tank had to offer, but I didn't have enough to get to the Oshetna River and back to pick up a hunter. Like a fool, I used the floatplane hand pump to suck up a big overflow puddle I'd made an hour earlier. Well, I drained it through a chamois and into a wing tank. To make a long story short, the gas was bad, the engine quit, and I had to make a forced landing on the tundra where I spent three nights freezing my ass. Since then, every time I spill some gas, I piss in it just so I won't be tempted to use it."

Gus muttered something about the Iranians doing the same thing in their oil but how it still always brings a better price than Alaskan crude.

Mica primed the engine a couple of times and hit the starter button on the old Cessna. In conjunction with a labored whine, the propeller made a half revolution and quit. Three more attempts produced similar results. I hopped from the plane; and with both hands on the prop, one quick downward spin produced a few coughs, some black smoke, and then a blast of air from the prop. As I climbed back aboard, Mica was working the throttle knob back and forth and, at the same time, yelling about the damned "new" battery that he'd just installed in 1975. They apparently didn't make them to last anymore.

We taxied up the road, spun the tail around, and roared back down the road. I hoped anyone else driving down the lane was as quick as Gus at taking to the ditch. We were airborne just after three, plenty of time to get where we'd planned and set up a quick base camp before dark.

Despite Mica's seemingly nonchalant attitude about his equipment and the apparent questionable airworthiness of old Delta, I had no reservations about flying with him. I'd spent a few hundred hours at the controls of light aircraft myself and had flown hundreds of additional hours with some of the best of Alaska's bush pilots. Mica was unquestionably one of the smoothest and safest pilots in the business. The engine purred as he twisted the fuel mixture knob toward lean.

We were cruising at an indicated one hundred and twenty knots at about eight hundred feet above the stunted spruce forests. Below us, the taiga undulated gently with the now-eroded moraines that forty-thousand-year-old glaciers had left behind. The impossibly green spruce was polka-dotted with low swales where permafrost lenses had warmed and melted, leaving untold thousands of catchment basins too wet to support evergreens. These boggy areas nurtured colonies of birch, now blazing with orange and yellow punctuation marks. The low-lying eroded ridgelines had better drained soils where even the spruce thinned out to a scattering of sentinel-like leftovers. Dwarf birch and blueberry filled in most of the gaps, and from our altitude, they lent an inviting carpeted understory. Where the soil was too rocky to support more substantial vegetation, ancient hoof- and claw-scarred trails were the only bare earth showing through carpets of lush caribou lichen, lending an appearance of off-white snow to the ground. This was the land of dreamers. The land of silent awe. This was Alaska.

Periodically, we saw moose in the boggy lakes that dotted the taiga. Trumpeter swans, once on the verge of extinction but now quite common, nested in the area and were beginning to congregate into loose groups of twenty or thirty individuals. The big white adult pairs were usually accompanied by three or four blue-gray cygnets. Countless thousands of ducks dotted the shallow lakes. In a few short weeks, the annual migrations in this country would be over. The ponds and lakes freeze quickly in the short daylight of autumn, and temperatures of fifty to sixty degrees below zero would push the ice deeper and deeper into the lakes. By February, some lakes would have their waters and occupants temporarily entombed by ice over five feet thick.

Caribou bands numbering from a dozen to fifty animals materialized before us then were gone in a flash beneath our slipstream. Following the "crash" of 1972 caused by overhunting and a few severe winters, the herd now numbered over thirty thousand head. Conservative management by the state Fish and Game Department enabled a timely comeback, while still allowing a controlled harvest. Gus and I had enjoyed some spectacular hunts a few miles west of here in previous years.

As we approached the mountains, the turbulence in the air thrashed us about, taking a toll on the aircraft as well as the occupants. Clouds hung low in the glacial valleys. Like jagged teeth of a giant carnivore, snow-laden peaks jutted through the clouds, nurturing a birthplace for the glaciers that provided the trickles of meltwater that would coalesce to form the South Fork of the Matanuska River. We flew up the braided river, and as the channel gave way to the Powell Glacier, we periodically began seeing sheep grazing the slopes below the snowline. As we continued up the glacier, the turbulence progressed toward violence.

It was beginning to appear that the weather forecasters were not being true to form. Through some strange quirk of nature, what they had predicted rapidly became reality. The farther up the glacier we proceeded, the more turbulent it became. The wind boiled over the mountains to the east of us, with telltale clouds of snow carried in the blizzard. About the time I noticed Mica was getting a bit nervous about the weather, he dipped a wing and swung the plane around, and we retreated north down the glacier.

As we reached the toe of the glacier, the wind diminished considerably. Mica, in his typical holler—which was now warranted—conveyed to us that we wouldn't be going to Futility Strip today. The old Alaskan pilot's adage was familiar to us all: "There's old pilots and there's bold pilots, but there ain't many old, bold pilots."

As we rounded the mountains and headed back east, Mica mentioned that he knew where a nice band of rams usually hung out late in the season, and we might as well try a hunt there. I quickly conveyed this to Gus in the backseat, who nodded his concurrence.

In a few more minutes, Mica swung the plane back south, and we headed across Tazlina Lake toward the glacier. A thick fog was forming on the lake, indicating the coolness of the autumn air. Where warmer, moist air off the lake met the dry, cold air slipping off the glaciers, it was common to see the fog buildup. We had no problem staying above the fog bank, and by the time we reached Tazlina Glacier, the ground was once again visible. Mica gently swung the plane toward Iceberg Lake and seemed surprised as the "lake" came into view. "That damned pond is about as predictable as a fart in a whirlwind!"

Apparently I was missing something. "What pond?" I asked.

"That's just it," hollered Mica. "About every three or four years the ice dam breaks away, melts, or whatever, and the two-mile lake drains out drier'n a popcorn fart!"

Looking closer, I could see the high-water mark where wave action had eroded the thin soil. Sure enough, where a sizable lake had been, there were now only dry rocks.

"This is young country," Mica continued. "The Wrangells still steam constantly from volcanic vents. Earthquakes are common occurrences, glaciers are carving up the mountains, and nothin' stays constant very long. It always seems like a fast-motion geology course . . . kinda excitin'."

We continued up the glacier, and within a few more minutes, my popping eardrums indicated our descent. As we got lower, it again became evident that the wind had the potential to create a sizable problem with landing.

Mica pointed south to a group of rugged spires among the ice fields.

"Your rams like to hole up on the east faces of those rocks. If this wind wasn't so squirrelly, we'd look 'em over, but if you can get in there, I'll guarantee you two pups some forty-inch sheep. Right now we better settle this bird down so's you an' Gus can get to huntin'."

It was always a real benefit to aerially look over the terrain you wanted to hunt, but in this case, I wasn't going to argue with Mica. The wind didn't allow us an up-close look at the country, and I wasn't about to push Mica into flying in a country he was uncomfortable with.

As we descended, I started looking for our landing site. The plane was equipped with oversized tundra tires, not skis or floats. As best I could tell, we were headed directly for a spur glacier that came into Tazlina Glacier from the east. My experience with glaciers was that they usually didn't provide the smoothest runways, but Mica didn't vary his course.

"You put this bird down here before?" I asked.

"Not right here, but a month ago I was flyin' this country, and there looked to be a respectable flat spot between a couple of crevasses that we can settle into without too much problem," Mica replied. "That is, if the dang wind ain't pushin' too hard one way or t'other."

We flew over the intended landing site low and slow, and Mica's experienced eye judged the possibilities. Another circle and Mica throttled back and pulled a few degrees of flaps. Unconsciously, I tightened my lap belt, and each air pocket we flew through squeezed my bladder a bit more.

I thought we were landing, but at the last second, Mica inched the yoke back, and we flew along a few feet over the ice as Mica counted loudly, "One, two, three, four, five, six, seven, eight, nine, ten, eleven, twelve, fourteen." At fourteen, a sizable crevasse opened beneath the wheels, and Mica again pulled back on the yoke, added power, and let off the flaps.

"A fourteen-count strip. Plenty of room to settle ol' Delta to a stop. We won't even need the grappling hook for this one," Mica joked as we regained airspeed and started another circle.

"What happened to thirteen?" I shouted.

"I ain't one to be superstitious, but why take the chance!"

As we circled for a landing, I wondered why Gus had been so uncharacteristically quiet in the backseat. A quick glance answered my question. All I could see was the bald spot on the top of Gus's head, with a big white barf bag held up by both hands and covering his face. I decided not to rub it in at this point but would certainly remember this momentous occasion to be used against him at a later, more opportune time.

As the oversized tundra tires touched down on the hard glacier ice, each minute crack was jolting, further reminding me that I'd forgot to empty my bladder. Mica immediately throttled back and stood on the brakes. Our airspeed at touchdown was probably no more than fifty miles per hour, but the slight downhill landing angle wasn't helping our efforts to stop. As the crevasse approached, our speed finally decreased enough to enable Mica to deftly swing the plane around 180 degrees, coasting uphill to a stop. Mica stopped the prop, and as he swung out of his door, I heard him mention something about cheating the grim reaper one more time.

Mica immediately went back and opened the cargo door and began dumping guns, tents, packs, and freeze-dried food out on the ice. I climbed out my side and promptly began getting rid of some used coffee. Gus slowly followed, not quite the boisterous, cheery partner I was accustomed to.

Mica grinned at Gus and said matter-of-factly, "Your eyes kinda look like two piss-holes in the snow. Sorry 'bout the bumpy flight."

Gus didn't respond.

"See you boys in ten days . . . sometime around noon" was Mica's remark as he climbed back aboard. He looked at me and continued, "You best take care of that little lady you're wet-nursin'. His green color don't blend in too well with rocks and ice."

Gus was finally feeling like he might live, and he responded simply by ejecting a brown stream of tobacco spittle down his chin. He stepped back a few inches so the drips didn't discolor his boots.

We waved as the Cessna lifted off in front of us. As soon as he gained a little airspeed, Mica wagged his wings and disappeared around the mountain.

THE HUNT

The first words out of Gus's mouth in the last hour were typical, and I knew the motion sickness was all but gone. "Shit! Left my damn windbreaker in the plane."

"Well, it'll have to keep my hat company. I'm sure they'll be all right," I said, also a tad irritated I'd left my good-luck baseball cap in the plane.

Although it was only six o'clock, the sun had disappeared behind the mountains west of us. We repacked the gear into our backpacks and transported it to the boulder-strewn moraine a quarter mile across the ice pack. The evening was spent locating a suitable camp. On every sheep hunt I've been on, the word "camp" is used loosely. The list of criteria for an acceptable camp is long and complicated. Therefore, Gus and I have never had one that was acceptable. We generally look for an area out of the wind, reasonably close to water (but yet out of the path of a downpour), and with a flat area devoid of boulders where we can pitch the sleeping tent.

As the sky transposed into darkness, the campstove and I produced the dinner, while Gus volunteered to find the "perfect" tent spot. Anyone familiar with hunting trips is painfully aware that the first meal is always the worst, simply because the taste buds haven't been properly deprived for the necessary amount of time. As the hunt progresses, hunger (or malnutrition) dictates that food bypass the regular mastication process in the mouth and go directly to the gut. In reality, the food quality undoubtedly declines with each meal, but I've never actually tasted anything after the second day.

On our previous trip, Gus was in charge of setting up the tent. That night, well after darkness had enveloped the basin, I hopped into my "fartsack" (Gus's name for a sleeping bag) and shivered some body heat into it while still in a sitting position. As I lay down, it was patently clear that good old Gus had planted a fist-sized rock directly under my lumbar region. The thin foam pad did little to smooth the terrain. As the night progressed, I became convinced that the lump was not mineral in nature but rather must have been animal or vegetable, capable of phenomenal growth. Before morning arrived, the lump had seemingly grown to the proportions of a well-fed porcupine. During the course of the next day, I managed to transplant the lump beneath Gus's sleeping bag and pad for the remainder of our short stay.

Five AM comes quickly in the mountains. Fortunately, five o'clock in September in these mountains brings not much more light than that found inside a cow. I had little trouble rolling over and dozing off again. By seven, Gus was up and purposefully banging aluminum pots to make sure I'd mosey out of the tent, at which time I was offered a steaming cup of gritty coffee.

Weather, always a topic of bleary early-morning discussions and arguments, was grim. Although little snow had fallen during the night, the temperature seemed about twenty, with a surreal light quality. It was calm as a road-killed skunk, and the glacier we were camped on seemed to go on and on forever. The white of the sky matched the white of the glacier, making it impossible to tell where one quit and the other started. The half mile to the stark black cliffs on the opposite side of the glacier was obscured by a white soup that you could almost cut with a knife.

"No huntin' for a while this fine autumn morning. Guess I got time to lighten the load a bit and fry up some flatcakes," Gus said.

"Your flatcakes, Gus, stretch the most vivid imagination. I've seen baseballs was flatter'n them cakes. Why don't you figure out how to build 'em itty-bitty, and we can go into business stuffin' 'em into shotgun shells. They'd damn sure be heavier'n lead shot, but probably just as toxic to the ducks that might be unfortunate enough to swallow one. Not complainin' though. You do the buildin', and I 'spect I can do the eatin'.

"How'd your beauty rest treat your carbuncles and age-warts?" I changed the subject before Gus could go into an hour-long discourse about his culinary prowess.

"I slept like a newborn calf just fresh dropped into a warm pile of soft cowshit. And yourownself?" he replied.

"Ditto, 'cept for the covey of porcupines . . ."

I chewed some more coffee, pulled my parka from its pillowcase, and shivered some heat into my body. Gus, meanwhile, continued to talk about weather, politics, and anything else that came to mind. That guy could keep himself entertained talking to ants.

Once the caffeine started circulating and the morning chill seemed to diminish somewhat, I busied myself by wandering down to the foot-wide stream to refill the coffeepot and other miscellaneous water containers we'd brought. As I dropped away from camp through the clouds, Gus's one-sided discussion with whomever continued. I doubt if he even realized I wasn't there to listen, and if he did notice I was gone, it probably wouldn't have made any difference anyhow. No chance of getting lost out here even in the soupy weather; Gus's diatribe was like a homing beacon for anybody within a quarter mile.

The grizzly stared through the fog, trying to focus. Her nose tested the leaden air for a hint of danger. Ears pointed toward the dark figure picking its way down to the stream. A low rumble from her throat caught the attention of her two yearlings, and they immediately responded by scurrying to her side and looking at the intruder.

I squatted down to fill the pots, hoping that the weather would lift today, and we could get on with the hunt. As my fingers quickly numbed in the icy glacial runoff and the coffeepot filled, the low woofing of the sow snapped me out of my reverie. At the same instant as my senses came to full alert and the hackles at my collar stiffened, I heard the unmistakable sound of clacking teeth. After a frantic couple of seconds of scanning my surroundings, I spotted the silhouette ghosting through the mist. Couldn't have been any farther than sixty yards. I must have been brain-dead to walk away from camp without my rifle. This situation had disastrous potential. The standoff lasted another thirty seconds or so, while the grizz decided her course of action. I had little input into her decision, and even smaller choice in the outcome of that decision.

I knew running was not an option. She knows I'm here. She hasn't yet decided whether to eat me or get the hell away. Damnit!

At that point she turned broadside, clacked her powerful jaws together a couple more times, and slapped the nearest cub in the flanks; and with a dozen or so muscle-rippling strides, the Toklat disappeared into the mist.

This encounter ended the way 99 percent of grizzly encounters do. I was apparently not perceived as an immediate threat to her cubs, herself, or her food supply; so she had no real need to defend any of the three. I was aware, on the other hand, that these interior grizzlies were not like the more complacent coastal brownies. Their food sources were limited, not having continuous runs of salmon upon which to dine. Winters were long and brutal, and from the time they emerge from their dens in late April or May until reentry in late October or early November, the "growing season" available to them was contracted. By necessity, they had to make do with limited food and a short season in which to lay down the necessary fat to carry them through. They were aggressive and often unpredictable. Fortunately for me, in this case, this particular sow decided against an easy meal.

I bent down to refill the spilled water containers and headed back up the boulders to the campsite. As I approached, I heard Gus's monologue continuing unabated. Putting the coffeepot on a suitable rock next to the baseball-sized dough balls on the single-burner stove, I began to tell Gus of the recent bruin encounter. "I'm pretty certain there's a bear or two around." I waited for him to nibble the bait, at which time I could really expound and, like a true hunter, expand the experience a bit.

"Yeah, that malnourished Toklat sow with the two scrawny yearlings?"

I shook my head, knowing the wind had just gone out of my sails.

"While you was out getting your morning's beauty rest," Gus continued, "she and those two delinquents of hers sauntered up this way, not more'n forty yards away. We engaged in a short conversation, at which time I pointed out to her that my rifle was pretty accurate at that range. She simply indicated my coffee was about to boil over and that she'd not appreciate that sort of toxic waste dumping in her backyard. After that, she rousted them two microbears of hers and faded down the hill. I meant to tell you to grab your smoke pole when you went for water, but you don't listen to me anyhow."

"Thanks a million, Gus," I said.

He knew he'd one-upped me again, and I knew he couldn't let that rest. He continued, "I 'spect we'd better keep our eyes peeled. She'll be back. By the way, anybody ever tell you how to peel your eyes. I've heard that stupid saying since I was a pup, and never did figure out how to peel my eyes. Sounds like it might hurt."

Gus wasn't looking for an answer; he was just on a roll and couldn't keep from jawing. I enjoyed just staring at the hardening lumps of flour in the frypan and listening, once in a while prompting Gus to continue.

"Eye-peeling aside," I said, "I agree that old sow will most likely be back this way. We could put a dab of sugar on those sinkers you're frying, scatter a few around the camp, and she'll wish she'd stayed a drainage or two away from here. If they don't kill her going in, I'm sure they'll stop her up coming out. She'll swell up like a snake-bit rat and probably explode bear guts and blood all over the tundra."

"Long's were on the subject of bears," Gus went on, "I ever tell you 'bout the time that ol' boar grizz chewed on my leg? Still got the scars."

"Yeah, Gus. I heard about twenty different versions of that escapade, an' if you'll remember, I was in the tent next to you when it happened, and you should also remember that it was a lost cub, an' it was your toe he sucked on, not your leg. I still think he probably mistook it for his mama's tit, only lookin' for some milk. My god, you can sure inflate a simple story."

"Well," continued Gus, "an old fart such as myself ought to be forgiven such slight memory lapses. Let's belly up to the kitchenette here, enjoy the weather, an' have our mornin's feast."

Back at the Meyers' place, the situation was not so lackadaisical. Anna had stopped by in the evening with some fresh blueberry pie, only to find no sign of her father. She left the pie in the refrigerator, found some three-day-old stew to feed the dog, and returned to town. Her father'd been tardy on many previous occasions for one reason or another, so she wasn't overly concerned. The weather was moving in, and she suspected her father had simply got caught in the squalls somewhere and was waiting it out. But the next morning she telephoned his place, still without results.

By noon, the clouds in the flats had lifted to two or three hundred feet, and Anna called several more times. She telephoned a few of the other area pilots to see if they'd heard anything from Mica. Again, nothing. Evening approached; and she drove back on out to the homestead, hoping, but only half expecting, to find her father elbows deep in a greasy airplane engine, harvesting what was left of the garden, or relaxing in front of the television. It wasn't the case.

Just before darkness settled over the Nelchina Basin, she'd figured out that the old Cessna 180, Delta, was the one missing. She checked the chalkboard and found that the two hunting parties that were to be picked up today had not been checked off the list. Apparently, yesterday afternoon, Mica had taken two sheep hunters to Futility Strip in the Chugach Mountains. He hadn't returned.

Following a fitful, largely sleepless night, Anna still waited for her father. By midmorning, she was definitely worried. She tried the other pilots again. Still nobody had heard a thing, but all three agreed to meet her at the homestead and try to figure out a search plan. The bush pilots in the basin, like the whole of Alaska, were a tight-knit group of individuals. One of their own was obviously stuck somewhere with a flat tire, a bent lift strut, an overturned plane, or worse; and each had been helped by the other at some point over the years. There was an unwritten, unspoken pact that bound them together. They were the best of the best at landing and taking off from impossible boulder fields, chasm-crossed glaciers, and minuscule river bars. With even the slightest hint of trouble, they responded by dropping other commitments and throwing in together.

Anna felt better as the last of the three assembled in the driveway, each with his respective SuperCub, and each with a sole purpose: to find Mica and his aircraft and do whatever was needed to get him back in the air. Two of the pilots, Tom and Lonny, were not much older than Anna. She'd grown up with them, periodically shared a beer and a pool game with them at the local roadhouse, and even, a couple of years back, had a short, hot, semiserious relationship with Tom. Both Tom and Lonny had flying experience way beyond their years that, nobody would contest, put them in the "bush pilot" class. They'd grown up with fathers who'd been glacier pilots and were flying SuperCubs solo before they'd had any idea about the intricacies of driving a car or other such mundane, civilized accouterment.

The third pilot was a short, wiry old fart who, like Mica, had migrated to Alaska after the Second World War. He'd honed his former fighter-pilot skills to a new edge, pushing the envelope ever wider with his beat-up Piper. Because of his age and accompanying wisdom, the youngsters deferred to him.

"Looks like you've done enough worrying for all four of us. D'you get any sleep last night?" he asked Anna.

"I don't know why I worry about that old bastard. He's probably just payin' me back for all the nights I kept him an' Mom awake. At least this time, though, I'll get to be the one to chew on his butt awhile when he gets back. I'm glad I ain't got any kids of my own yet. Takin' care of him is a full-time occupation.

"Anyway, seems two days ago his last flight was with a couple guys, one named Lander, to a place he calls Futility Strip. I'm not even sure where that is. He took Delta, his blue one-eighty. That's about all I know."

"Pop" Howard took up where Anna had left off, looking at Tom and Lonny. "You boys know where the strip is, you know the airplane, and you also remember the piss-poor weather that moved in that evening." It was more of a statement than a question, and getting nods from both the others, he continued, "For now, let's center the search between here and the strip. I'll go in and see if I can roust those hunters and see what they might know. Chances are, Mica'll be sittin' tight with them if he's got something broke. Let's stay on 118.8 if you both got radios, but check the emergency frequency from time to time, in case he's tryin' to signal. Anna, you go get some rest so's you can do some real ass-chewin' on that father of yours when we get him back here."

"Once we hit the drainage," Tom spoke up, "I'll stay to the west side. Lonny, why don't you take the east, and Pop can run up the center."

"Sounds good to me," responded Pop. The ever-quiet Lonny simply nodded in quick agreement.

"Thanks much, guys," said Anna. "You all know where the gas is if you need to fill up. Go ahead an' help yourselves. Anything I can do here?"

The three pilots had already headed off toward their Cubs; only Pop was hesitating at Anna's question. "Yeah, Anna. Would you call the Shrew, tell her where I'm at, and tell her I might be late for supper?"

"Sure thing, Pop."

Less than an hour later, all planes were back on the ground at Mica's place. The weather in the mountains had dictated an early retreat before the strip was reached. "Come on in for something to eat," Anna said, trying, without much success, to hide her disappointment.

"First off," Pop replied, "this bum weather's probably good news, Anna. Mica's probably holed up waitin' for the scud to lift a bit. I 'spect this evening he'll come moseyin' back. Meanwhile, I don't have anything pressin' this afternoon. You know if Mica's got other hunters out that need a ride back here?"

"His chalkboard lists a couple guys that were supposed to be picked up yesterday up the Big O. Today, there's a group of three that're on Kosina Lake that need to be picked up." As an afterthought, she added, "Fortunately, I didn't see anybody on the list that wanted to go in yesterday or today."

Tom volunteered, "The weather looks pretty good up toward the Oshetna and Kosina country. We can probably run up there and pick up those two on the O before dark. Assumin' they got a couple moose, though, we better take three Cubs. Lonny, you got the time today?"

"Sure. No problem."

Within minutes, all three planes were again airborne, headed northwest. Anna busied herself in her father's kitchen, putting together a two-gallon pot of moose stew and sourdough biscuits. She mentally cussed her father, along with the three pilots who'd just departed. *They're so damned independent,* she thought. *Always think they can take on the world. I start running out of fingers and toes when I think of all the one's I've known in the past that've augured in. They have this romantic idea that it'll always happen to the other guy, never to them.*

As darkness began shrouding the basin, the drone of an airplane temporarily lifted her spirits. She dropped the stew ladle and flew out the door. It was, she thought dejectedly, the sound of a Cub, not the one-eighty. Within ten minutes, Lonny and Pop had taxied up thc driveway, accompanied by the hunters. Tom straggled in fifteen minutes later with a load of moose meat, and everybody pitched in to get the hunters and their meat into a pickup, which departed down the lane just as the last light of day faded into darkness.

There was little of the ordinary banter between pilots. Mica was now two full days late. The fact was on everybody's mind but remained unspoken. Lonny was in the washroom, cleaning up for stew and biscuits. Anna could hear Pop in the living room, talking with Flight Service about the coming weather. Tom was seated at the table, fresh coffee steaming from his mug.

"Anna, you know Mica's probably just waitin' out the weather," he began. "I know it's easier said than done, but you gotta try'n relax. He'll be back tomorrow. Meanwhile, we'll make sure'n get those other hunters outta Kosina Lake, an' your Dad can take up where we left off."

"Tom, something's wrong this time. Really wrong. The way you guys are actin', you know it too. Damnit, why didn't I leave this miserable basin years ago. The ones we grew up with that had any sense are all gone. Anchorage. Seattle. Idaho. Why didn't I make something of my life and get the hell outta here."

"Seems to me," Tom replied, "you did go lookin' elsewhere an' ended up back here. We were born in this country, and we were born *to* this country. You could no more exist somewhere else than I could. This country, even with all its downfalls, is in your blood. Your *soul.* Just look out there. That's clean air, that's crystal clean water, that's our *life.*"

He was standing by her now and reached up to wipe a tear streaking Anna's cheek. She turned, embraced him, and sobbed into his chest.

Over dinner, of what little talking there was, flying weather was the main topic. The storm was predicted to hang in for a few more days, but by noon tomorrow, the ceilings should lift somewhat. The three pilots pretty well finished the stew and biscuits and polished off the blueberry pie. Anna picked at her meal, with not really much of an appetite.

Agreeing to meet there again tomorrow at about noon, they said their good nights and slipped out into the night. Tom was the last out the door, giving Anna a solid, understanding hug at the door.

She looked up at him. "I appreciate what you guys are doing. As a favor, Tom, I really don't want to stay in this old house tonight alone."

The first day was a relatively relaxed one for Gus and me. Following the bear encounters of the morning, we passed the time uneventfully waiting for the weather to lift before we could head out in search of a couple of rams. I listened to Gus talk about everything from the miserable price of wolverine pelts to the ever-diminishing size of chocolate bars. It always amazed me how he transformed into an entirely different person when away from the city job.

I lost several million dollars, by Gus's estimate, while playing cribbage with him. We studied what we could see of the terrain, trying to decide the best tactics to chase sheep when the weather broke. By late evening, Gus was pleasantly snoring, with the porcupines complacently playing their rugby games beneath *his* sleeping pad.

The morning of day 2 brought some improvement in the weather. Below us about a thousand feet, a cloud layer socked in the valley. Looking up the glacier, cloud bases were maybe two thousand feet up the mountains. Although not perfect, it was time to get started. By midmorning, we were packed up and had our bellies full of coffee grounds, reconstituted eggs, and hardtack bread.

Three hours later, we had the spotting scope set up at the base of the unnamed collection of glacier-covered mountains that Mica had indicated usually held the rams.

"Even with the clouds, I got about forty sheep in sight," Gus remarked around the several fists of trail mix in his mouth. "Course, they're all ewes an' lambs, 'cept maybe that group of six up there." He indicated with a nod and an outstretched finger toward the head of the main canyon.

"The way those six are actin', I'll bet you're right," I put in. "I think we can work about halfway up the west flank there without spookin' any of those other groups, which ought to put us within about a half mile of those rams, an' we can get a better look."

Indicating again with a slight nod toward the mountain, Gus continued, "Let's work our way up the bottom to that second side drainage, then up that creek about halfway to the ridgeline. That ought to keep us outta sight and probably downwind. That'll give us a good vantage point, assumin' the clouds don't roll in on top of us." We usually discussed such particulars with a map in hand, but because of the weather-forced change in hunting locations, we had no such convenience.

Another four hours and about a thousand feet or so of gained elevation later, we'd positioned ourselves to get to the approximate point Gus had picked out earlier. Again, the spotting scope was set up, and Gus was peering toward the small band of rams about six or seven hundred yards from us, at about the same elevation.

"At this point, I can only see four of 'em, but at least one, maybe two, are reasonable rams." The sheep were still loosely grouped, grazing in more or less the same patch of alpine bunchgrass. "You better take a look," Gus continued.

I moved low across the lichen-covered scree and looked through the scope. "Yeah, I agree at least one of 'em's a nice one. Let's sit tight awhile and see if we can wait the other two out. They gotta be right there close."

"I ain't one to argue about sittin' tight," Gus agreed. "Why is it every time we chase these damn sheep, I swear to myself I'll never, ever, hunt these damn mountains again? It's gotta be the most miserable weather, the worst food, the lumpiest sleeping accommodations, and the toughest packs imaginable. I guess the clean water and winnin' all that cribbage money from you makes me keep comin' back. That an' the fact I can whine all I want and dribble tobacco juice down my chin and nobody gives me grief."

"There's one of those other sheep," I broke in, just as Gus was getting rolling. "I can just see his back . . . there he comes. He looks about like a twin of the bigger sheep in the band. I'd guess 'em both at about thirty-eight inches. Hard to tell at this range which one's got heavier bases."

At this point, we needed the break. The spur ridge we were on was well enough out of sight where we could peer over with the scope and watch their movements without being seen ourselves. The winds were not uncomfortable and were in our favor regarding the rams in question. It wasn't raining or snowing, and it felt good just whispering back and forth, watching the sheep do sheep things.

"I guess we could get off our butts and go tip over one of those rams," I ventured.

"You sure are eager to punch your tag and start to work, aren't ya," Gus replied. "We got another eight or nine days in these hills, and you want to make a cold carcass outta the first decent sheep you lay eyes on."

"Well, there ain't no easier time, nor better weather than what we got here right now. I think we can work a stalk on those boys from the ridgeline on top, an' we can at least take a better look-see at what kind of headgear they're packin'. We'd have to come at 'em from in the clouds, though. We couldn't see them until we get about a hundred yards from 'em, but at the same time, they couldn't see us either."

"Well, it's pushin' five o'clock already. By the time we make the ridge and come back down on them sheep, assumin' they stay put, it'll be oh-dark-thirty. That, or we can slide back down this mountain and set a decent camp at the forks where the sheep can't see us. They'll be waitin' for us tomorrow mornin', an' you can throw all your bullets at 'em then."

What Gus had said made sense. Darkness would envelop the mountains in less than three hours, and getting caught in that darkness without camp preparations was something I didn't want to chance at this juncture of the trip.

"Let's just sit tight a few more minutes, and see if we can get a look at that sixth animal. I suspect you're right, we can always chase 'em tomorrow," I put in.

Twenty minutes later, all six sheep were visible. The straggler wasn't anything to brag about, but I still liked the look of the two larger rams. However, Gus's prodding, as well as my better judgment, dictated that we sneak back down the mountainside and establish a reasonable spike camp in the creek bottom. Tomorrow would come soon enough.

Well before light, Tom rolled over and took in the simple beauty of Anna's unclad body. Their pent-up desires for each other, as well as a rational form of tension release from the frustrations of the past two days, had resulted in long, tender lovemaking during the night, followed by deep, dreamless sleep that they both welcomed. It felt good to be beside her again, Tom thought as she stirred next to him, snuggling closer in the morning chill.

"I'd better get the coffee on, Tom," she said a few minutes later. "I'd like to just lounge around in this bed with you all morning, but Pop and Lonny'll be along pretty soon, I suspect. What I really want to hear is that damned old one-eighty taxiing up to the gas shed."

They both got up and dressed, heading downstairs to start the day. Anna busied herself in the kitchen while Tom worked on his plane in the morning twilight, fueling it up and conducting his routine preflight checks. Twenty minutes later, he returned to the house, where he was met with a steaming cup of coffee and a sincere, almost frantic, embrace.

"Anna, now may be the wrong time and place, but I'll ask anyway. Was last night just a convenience for you, having me stay?"

"I just don't know, Tom. I can't say that I haven't missed you the past couple years. You're right, now may not be the best time to ask. Just give me some time. Let's get through the next couple days and see what happens." She turned, hesitated, then turned back and added, "Thanks . . . for what you're doing, Tom. For everything."

As they entered the kitchen, the phone rang, and Anna grabbed it off the wall. “Oh, good morning, Pop . . . . Yeah, he’s here, want to talk to him?”

“Morning, Pop . . . . Yeah, I guess you could say that . . . . Okay, sounds good. We’ll plan on about noon. Thanks. You’ll get ahold of Lonny and see what he’s got going today? . . . Okay, see you then.”

Tom put on a somewhat sheepish grin as he hung up the phone. “Pop’ll be here about noon. He says the weather should be improving a bit by midday. He also wondered why I was out here so early this morning. Said he tried my place, without getting an answer.”

“My god, Tom. It’s not like we’re sixteen anymore.” She went on, doing her best to sound serious, “I’ll tell him when he gets here that it’s his turn tonight.”

After a quick breakfast, Tom fired up Mica’s floatplane, a well-used blue-and-silver Cessna 206, and headed northwest to pick up the hunting party on Kosina Lake. All went without incident, and after two trips for the hunters and their meat, he was back to the homestead by eleven. The cloud ceilings, as predicted, had started to lift; and by the time Pop and Lonny had arrived, it looked as if the search for Mica could begin in earnest.

“Same plan as yesterday morning?” Tom looked at Pop.

“Yeah, I’ll take the middle and you guys take the flanks. I got some pretty serious tools and parts loaded, and I think we’ll be able to fix a bent landing gear or a dinged prop if that’s what’s holding him up. The last thing we need’s another bent airplane up there, so both of you be careful.” As an afterthought, Pop continued, “I don’t think Mica uses the radio in the one-eighty, assumin’ it’s even got one. With the weather liftin’ like this, he may be headed our way, so keep a lookout for him comin’ back.”

In another ten minutes, they were all airborne, heading toward the mountains. Once they reached the Matanuska drainage, the canyon was relatively narrow, and they could keep each other in sight. Pop was the first one to reach the gravel outwash they called

Futility Strip. He circled once then dropped the Cub down onto the gravel. Tom and Lonny searched upstream of the strip a couple of miles, finding nothing. As Lonny continued the search pattern, Tom flew back down and landed to talk with Pop.

Tom pulled the lean knob, and the prop wound down as Pop walked up. “I know it’s rained and snowed a bit in the past couple days,” Pop said, “but I don’t see as Mica ever even landed here. None of these tracks look like they’ve been made in the past week or two, an’ what’s here looks to be Cub tracks, not one-eighty. Let’s walk around a bit an’ see if we can find any indication of a fresh camp. You guys see anything up the crick?”

“Not a thing, Pop.”

“Damn! I was hopin’ he’d be sittin’ right here with a bent gear and a hang-dog look on his face. This is shapin’ up to be serious.”

The next three hours was spent walking around the strip and flying the immediate area before the three pilots returned to Mica’s homestead. Late afternoon found them around the kitchen table once again.

“There’s just no sign of him,” Pop stated the obvious. “It’s been three full days, there’s no reports from the satellites about ELTs clicking, and the weather shouldn’t be holdin’ him up anymore. We better make it official an’ get the Feds involved.” The telephone call giving the particulars would bring in the military, the State Troopers, and a plethora of private pilots, in an organized, systematic search for the missing plane and its occupants.

In the mountains the next morning dawned cloudy and blustery, but the rains and snows were again holding off. Typical sheep hunting weather. The temperature hovered somewhere around freezing, but not wholly uncomfortable. Gus and I were moving back up the mountainside by nine. Several small bands of sheep were visible, but the ram group of yesterday evening had disappeared. Our game plan for the day was to return up the spur ridge and eventually gain the main ridge where we could glass not only the valley we had made camp in, but the next drainage over as well.

By midafternoon, we had again spotted the band of six rams up a side canyon and redirected our efforts to approaching them once again. The going was treacherous, as it nearly always was in these mountains, compounded by wet scree, in places still frozen from the night's frost. Our progress was slow but deliberate, and with every hundred yards we gained, we'd pause and pick another route across the terrain in front. We'd finally got the band below us, always a judicious tactic when hunting sheep. They rarely seemed to spend much time scanning for dangers above themselves. Unless the squirrelly mountain winds turned against you or insecure footing resulted in dislodging a boulder, a stalk from above was the best bet.

We sidehilled around the mountain, once coming upon a small, almost vertical drainage near the base of a huge avalanche chute. Scattered bones and patches of white hair littered the creek bed. It was obvious a group of rams had attempted to cross the chute sometime during a previous winter and had been swept along to their deaths when the avalanche ensued. We found a heavy-based, forty-two-inch ram skull lying partially submerged in the creek, battered and bleached, with one horn porcupine-chewed near the tip.

Again, it was after five o'clock when we were close enough to the rams to plan our final stalk.

"Under good circumstances, I 'spect it'd take us near three hours to get back to camp," Gus began. "We got a few options we better discuss 'fore we go tippin' over one of them rams."

"Yeah, we're pushin' the light once again, and I don't really want to spend the night working back to camp in the dark."

"Well, like I said, we got options. We can drop off right now and not have too much trouble makin' camp. We can work this stalk out an' thump one of them rams then siwash it right there on the mountain. If we take that one, it'll definitely be dark 'fore we're done caping and opening him up to cool. I guess we can tip one over, drop the guts, move the meat a ways down into the bottom, and try'n make it back to camp in one piece. Then we can come on up here first thing tomorrow; shoo away the bears, wolverines, and ravens; and get the meat back to camp."

I agreed, to a point. "Let's take door number 3. I'd opt to hurl a chunk of lead into that nice ram, then we can move the meat away from the gut pile. I think we can get him down to the crick bottom before dark, and once we're on the drainage, the return to camp won't be quite as bad as the going up here. It's clearing a bit, meaning it may not get dark quite so quick this evening, but also means it'll be colder'n a Nome well-digger's ass in January tonight."

Gus apparently concurred with the plan. "I'd just as soon spend the night back at camp. Sleepin' out here tonight would be like sittin' on top of McKinley in December, outta tobacco, wearin' nothin' but a wet jockstrap an' both kneecaps shot off."

"Damn, Gus. You sure got a way with words." I chuckled.

"Well, we best stop jawin' and get to killin'," said Gus. "I 'spect you want first shot?"

"Thanks, Old Man, but if you'll remember, I got the first chance three years ago, and made the most of it. I believe it's your turn."

"Thanks, Kid."

It took Gus less than 30 minutes to work himself into position for a 150-yard shot. As I watched the sheep through binoculars from my vantage point above them, I saw the big ram jerk and immediately go down. About the same time as the ram hit the turf, I heard the loud report from Gus's rifle. It was a clean kill, the ram never sensing danger. The other five sheep, as if choreographed for this event, banded together and bolted, stringing out single file and running across the scree. They had no clue as to the whereabouts of the danger; but, like mountain sheep everywhere, they gained altitude fast. I sat motionless, watching them run directly at me.

Gus and I had discussed this situation many times. I had been presented a perfect opportunity to take another ram. However, it was obvious that Gus had one down, and we had plenty of work with that one animal. We'd agreed on previous trips that one sheep at a time was plenty. I hunkered down and enjoyed the scene of the five sheep barreling past me at less than forty yards. The largest ram was trailing, and he stopped momentarily to scan the surroundings, I assumed to get a bearing of where the danger was coming from. We both remained motionless, the predator and the prey, looking directly at each other. He spun in an instant, heading up to the nearest escape cover in the crags and the clouds. The most overworked adjective of the upcoming generation was the only word that came to mind—awesome!

I folded the tripod, shouldered my pack frame, and, in another twenty minutes, was standing with Gus, admiring the beautiful snow-white ram.

"Nice shot, Old Man."

"Yeah." He spit a brown stream of tobacco juice, about half of which ended up on his chin and shirt. "Even a blind hog gets an acorn every once in a while."

We double-timed it to stay ahead of the approaching darkness, not wanting to complicate our way down the mountain. It was important that we proceed quickly before darkness descended; but Gus sat, pulled a plastic pint bottle from his pack, and poured a capful of Wild Turkey. As he poured it onto the rocks, he said, "First one's for you, sheep. I hope you had a good life in these mountains, and hope you got lots of little offspring behind ya. Thanks for the memories you're providin'." With that, Gus held the pint out for me. I quickly downed a gulp and handed it back to Gus. He too tipped the bottle to his lips, held the thick liquor in his mouth awhile, and swallowed it down.

It took almost an hour to rough-cape the sheep; remove the lower legs, guts, and skull; put the quarters into meat bags; and rope everything onto the two pack frames. Ravens, those ubiquitous scavengers of the mountains, had found us and croaked nearby waiting to clean up the entrails once we'd departed. It was already approaching twilight as we shouldered the sixty-pound packs and headed slowly and meticulously down the slope.

We'd inched our way downhill a couple hundred yards and were skirting the top of a sheer rock wall when Gus, behind me, stepped on a rock that apparently gave way under his foot. I spun around when I heard the commotion. Gus was sliding on his butt, feetfirst, down the steep pitched scree, trying to grab whatever he could to slow his descent. There was no time for me to do anything. No Hollywood screams or mad dashes to save my friend. In an instant, he was over the cliff, the sounds of rocks against rock, and dust swirling up from below. I hadn't moved more than a few feet.

"Gus! Damnit, GUS!" Nothing . . .

I let down my pack frame, found solid footing below me to the lip of the face, and inched down. Several yards below the base of the drop-off, I could see the contorted form. I called—no, screamed—down to him. No response. Frantically, I worked my way another couple hundred yards to where the face petered out and managed to get down and around the base, back to where Gus lay sprawled among the boulders.

As I approached, I saw no movement. Fearing the worst, I dropped my rifle and touched Gus's face. With that, he grimaced, and one eye painfully squinted open. "Wondered when you'd finally catch up. I found a shortcut and just been loungin' here waitin' for you. Figured you'd be scared of the dark if I left you back here alone." The pain in his voice was evident, but Gus played the tough guy.

"Damnit, Gus. You're beat to hell." I immediately began assessing the obvious damage. "Can you move at all?"

"Hell, not more'n a minute ago, I was assumin' you were an angel, come to fly me off these rocks. You're a disappointment for an angel, Kid. Now you're wantin' me to move by myself?"

Facial scrapes and lacerations and a bloody, bent nose looked like superficial injuries, although one side of his face was already swollen, and blood had pooled beneath his head. He was lying on his back, head slightly downhill, which was probably good to slow the shock that was inevitable, probably already setting in. His right leg was obviously broken at, or just below, the knee, bleeding badly through his jeans, and twisted grotesquely underneath him. Internal injuries were a probability. His shallow breathing was raspy, and each breath seemed to elicit a pulpy, weak cough. The whole situation looked grim.

We were a couple of miles from camp. It was getting dark. Soon, the mercury would drop well below freezing. Neither of us had brought gear to spend the night away from camp. It was six days, at least, before Mica would return. My mind raced.

"Gus, your leg's broke bad. Can you feel what else is hurting?"

"I . . . I feel like a roadkill, Kid. But yeah, I can feel my right leg . . . it ain't quite right. I hurt all over. I guess that's the good part . . . At least my back or neck ain't broke 'cause I'm sure receivin' all the hurt messages to my noggin."

"I got no choice then, Gus. I gotta move you. Get your leg put back in line, at least." As gently as possible, I lifted his upper leg and pulled the lower part into, more or less, a natural position. Gus grunted a few times but made a feeble attempt to help. His arms appeared scraped and bruised, but workable.

"That's a bit better, partner . . . Damn, I'm tired and cold. This don't look good, Kid. I'm fadin' fast." With that, he laid his head back down on the rocks and passed out.

The ravens screamed, and flies buzzed around the coagulated blood on Gus's pant leg. The breeze had stopped, and I shivered as the sweat cooled beneath my shirt. Darkness was only minutes away. I lifted Gus's head and found a four-inch gash behind his ear, still flowing blood. While he remained unconscious, I made a dressing from my shirt and quickly tied it around his head, which seemed to slow the bleeding. I took an extra cotton game bag from my pack and put it beneath his head and wrapped my light parka over his body. Up the boulder field ten yards lay Gus's pack frame, bent and banged. I retrieved his coat, gently wrapping his legs. The labored, gurgled breathing continued, so I took another chance and eased him around so he was more or less lying flat. It seemed to help.

My next chore was obvious. In the half-light remaining, I untied the sheep meat from my pack frame and scrambled down the mountain to a scraggly stand of willows in the bottom. I frantically broke, cut, and scavenged any burnable twig I could find, filled the water bottle, and headed back up the slope. It was probably two hours later as I groped my way back to Gus. The sky had begun clearing, and the stars and aurora shed enough light to help me back, although the treacherous footing and steep hillside made it slow. Dreading what I would find, I eased down next to Gus. My palm on his forehead, to my relief, brought him around once more.

"You ain't no cheechako, Kid . . . You know better'n to be traipsin' around these hills . . . in the dark."

"You just rest, Gus. We needed some firewood, and I got it. We'll both need it before the night's over. Here, have some water. I'll have tea going directly."

With some relatively dry bunchgrass from between the rocks, I got a small blaze going, but the meager willow twigs didn't produce much heat, and the crackle and light didn't do much to alter my perspective. Gus's body temperature, I found, had dropped dramatically. Once the water can was situated near the fire, I lay down on the rocks, wrapping Gus and me together in an attempt to share the heat from my strenuous trip up from the creek bottom. Just the slight movement of unwrapping the coats and bundling us up together was traumatic for Gus. He shook weakly, wracked by pain from a thousand sources.

"Kid," he started, more of a weak whisper now than a voice, "thanks for all the . . . the good times, huh . . . I'm busted up bad . . . an' don't think I'll be . . . be goin' much further. Look up there . . . Look at those stars a'twinklin' . . . northern lights a'dancin' . . ."

"We got lots of trips ahead of us, Gus, just lay quiet and—"

"No . . . no sense pretendin', Kid," he cut me off. "This is my last hunt. Tell Mattie I love her. Promise . . . promise me you'll take my pup too . . . take my pup from her an' hunt the hell outta her . . . You . . . you been a fine partner, Kid."

The first sun in days peeked through the eastern sky as the team assembled for the search. It did little to cheer the outlook of Anna or Tom, or the rest of the searchers, for that matter. The Rescue Coordination Center in Anchorage had been notified, and the suits had shown up to organize and take part in conducting the search.

Military aircraft were deployed with sensitive radio equipment that could, it was boasted, hear a faint emergency locator transmitter from five hundred miles away. The roadhouse at the Glacier Lodge was converted to a headquarters, and maps were thumbtacked to every wall. Satellite links were arranged, so ELT "hits" could be monitored and telephone service could be maintained. A grid pattern was set up for the searchers, all were given a map depicting each pilot's respective search area, fuel tanks were provided, and radio frequencies were discussed. Pop was the local "contact," a task he took well to, knowing Mica so well, knowing the country even better, and it helped having a military background. He could maintain a certain amount of control when the bureaucracy stumbled.

By one o'clock, all pilots, including Pop, Tom, and Lonny, had assembled for the initial briefing. All were somber and attentive, receiving their instructions for deployment locations. Besides the three "locals," the Alaska State Troopers had sent two fish and wildlife Protection Officers, familiar with the country. A military C-130 (Hercules) was momentarily departing the airbase near Anchorage to assist in the search. Three civilian search and rescue pilot/observer teams were present.

At two o'clock, the last plane departed the gravel runway.

By seven thirty, all had returned and were assembled in the roadhouse for the day's debriefing. Nothing had been found, except the remnants of an old crash site near Sheep Mountain that caused a momentary flood of excitement but was quickly discounted. Hundreds of square miles had been scrutinized, and the Herc had covered thousands more in its search for an ELT signal. Nothing.

I had no idea what to do at this point. It was morning, frosty, windy, and miserable. The weather was the least of my worries. The small fire had run out of wood sometime during the night. I really didn't care. I was numb. Not from cold so much as from Gus's death. He shook and mumbled whispers for several hours then drifted off. I'd asked myself *why* a thousand times. Why had we pushed the darkness? Why had he taken such a heavy load of meat? Why hadn't I found a better route? Why hadn't I been able to help? Why? *Why?*

I moped, sobbed, cursed throughout the day. Despair, anger, frustration. I had no motivation to take care of basic needs. Warmth. Food. Taking care of my partner. My dead partner.

It was evening when reality struck. It came in the form of a squall. Cold, gusty winds. Heavy, horizontal snow. I gradually realized Gus's face was no longer visible. His stiff form was there, but snow was no longer melting on his face. My own coat, hanging loose around my shoulders, was stiff with frozen sleet and snow. I was shaking violently, huddled on the rock beside Gus with my legs tucked underneath me. My hands were unworkable, feet numb.

It took several minutes, accompanied by uncontrollable shaking, to stand and get the circulation going again. I alternately slipped, lurched, and tumbled, once again, down to the bottom of the drainage. It took what seemed an hour and virtually all my matches to get a small fire going, again relying on pencil-diameter sticks for fuel. Despite the rigors of the downhill climb, my fingers still refused to function with any reliability. The snow squalls pounded me relentlessly, but at least I'd become cognizant of the fact that I now needed to take care of myself.

I huddled by the little fire throughout the night, alternately dozing and then rummaging nearby in the fresh snow for sticks in an effort to maintain my meager but lifesaving fire. As dawn broke, I had become aware enough of the situation to know that I needed to return to the spike camp, attempt to get warm and dry, eat, sleep, and regroup. What should have been a two-hour stroll down the relatively gentle drainage turned out to be another five- or six-hour nightmare. My feet were still numb in the frozen boots, and my legs were weak from the cold and lack of nutrition. The snow-laden rocks were treacherous, and I stumbled and fell countless times. Clouds in the mountains mimicked the ebb and flow of the tides, raising momentarily, then angrily plunging back down the slopes, only to lift grudgingly back upward. Showers, changing to rain instead of snow, sporadically added to the misery.

Reaching the snow-laden tent in late afternoon, I was thankful bears hadn't visited and wreaked havoc with the outfit. One thing had finally gone right. It was all I could do to remove my boots and parka, shiver into my sleeping bag, and immediately slump into a stupor-like sleep.

The droning sound of a SuperCub, as well as an insatiable thirst, brought me awake within a couple of hours. I scrambled out of the tent and, standing in wet, mud-caked socks in the five-inch snow, was only able to watch and wave my arms frantically as the Cub departed, only two or three hundred feet off the deck, down the valley. I started for the nearby stream, stumbled, and fell. I got up and immediately stumbled again. What the hell was wrong with my feet? Sitting, covered once again with the wet sticky snow, I brushed off my feet. They were swollen to half again their normal size. Terrified, I quickly pulled off the stretched socks. What should have been wrinkled pink toes looked like ghostly white sausages. Both ankles were puffy white, without the normal contours. In the diminishing light, I crawled to the stream, drank for what seemed like endless minutes, and quickly crawled back to the tent, exhausted with the effort, and scared of the sickly condition of my feet. Once again, total exhaustion, then sleep, overtook me within seconds of bundling up in the bag.

The second day of the official search again revealed nothing. New search areas were assigned, and yesterday's areas were again scrutinized. Tom had requested that he be assigned the upper Nelchina Glacier country, and he and Pop headed that way. The clouds and turbulent wind shears made flying and searching difficult and dangerous, but they stuck to the search throughout the day. Toward the headwaters, unfortunately, the fresh snow and wind would have covered any wreckage or obliterated any potential tracks. They didn't spend much time there, assuming it futile. Unbeknownst to me, it was Tom's search plane I'd seen departing back down the glacier.

"We can't count him out yet," Tom quietly and matter-of-factly said to Anna. They were sitting at the kitchen table, Anna with dark circles beneath her eyes, her chin resting despondently in her palm.

"I know that, Tom. And I'm not about to give up. With all you guys out scouring the hills, you gotta find something that's gonna give us some hope sooner or later. They didn't just vanish. Where in God's name did they go? What the hell's happened?"

"I wish I knew . . . man, I wish I knew . . ."

"Let me make you something to eat. That's the least I can do to repay you for what you're doing for me," she said.

Tom reached across the small wooden table and took Anna's hand. "I'm not doing this just for you, Anna. I'm doing this for Mica, and for those two hunters, and for their families, and for myself. I owe Mica a lot. I don't know how many times he's dropped what he was doing to help me out. He's helped just about everybody in this basin at one time or another. We need him here."

They sat silent for several more minutes, before Anna squeezed Tom's hand and rose from the table. "I baked some potatoes and a moose roast earlier today. Let me heat it up for you."

"Yeah, thanks. That'd be real good . . . Can I use your telephone? I gotta check with my brother to see if he'll pick up a couple moose hunters I got out over by Tangle Lakes. I'd better check on the weather for tomorrow too."

"Sure, help yourself. I've been meaning to ask too, is there anything I can do while you're out there boring holes in the sky?"

Tom answered on his way to the phone in the next room. "Not that I can think of, Anna, but thanks for asking."

Just as Tom was hanging up the phone a few minutes later, Anna came in with a plate of steaming moose roast with all the trimmings. "There is one thing you can do for me, Anna."

"What's that? Name it."

"Take care of yourself. I mean, you gotta keep your health through this. You haven't had a decent night's rest in a week, and I never see you eating. You're so skinny now you probably have to stand up twice to make a decent shadow. We'll find him." After a long pause, Tom added, "And I hope you'll keep taking care of me."

Anna gently put the steaming plate on the coffee table and straddled Tom in the straight-backed chair. She put her arms around his neck and leaned her forehead on his. "Let's take care of each other," she whispered.

An hour later, the only light that entered the living room was that spilling through the kitchen door, coming from a small bulb above the stove. Tom again watched the rhythmic beat of Anna's heart and the perfect, seemingly untroubled rise and fall of her breasts as she lay sleeping on the carpet where they had urgently, passionately, made love. He pulled on his jeans and found a blanket on the couch that he gently laid over her. Thoroughly famished, he ate the now-cold dinner she'd prepared then helped himself to another plateful. Thus satiated, he stooped, picked up Anna, and carried her upstairs to bed. Entwined in each other's arms, they were sound asleep in minutes.

At the end of the third day of the official search, the seventh day since Mica had left the homestead, there was again no news. No news, in this case, was bad news.

Gus's wife, Mattie, had been contacted to see, by chance, if Gus had returned or said anything about where he and Charlie were planning to hunt. No, she couldn't recall him saying where they were headed, other than they'd be flying out with Mica Meyers. Why were they asking, anyhow? Gus wasn't scheduled to return for another three or four days.

"Well," the officer explained, "Mr. Meyers hasn't returned from the flight on which he'd dropped them off. As you may have seen in the papers, there's a search being conducted for his airplane and him. We're just checking out the possibilities, ma'am. No need for alarm."

No need for alarm, my eye, she thought. "What you're saying is that the plane may have crashed and my husband may have been on it. Right?"

"Well, there is that remote possibility. We'll contact you when we have any information at all, Mrs. Harms. Please feel free to call me if you've got questions," he finished, handing her his gold-embossed, logo-studded Alaska State Trooper business card.

My god, she thought as she closed the door and sat down. *Did Charlie's girlfriend know anything? Had she even been contacted? What kind of a dolt was that who was just here? Had about as much tact as a freight train.* Mattie decided to call Sarah, a fortunate decision.

Trying to contain her immediate anger, Mattie telephoned. "Sarah? Hello, this is Mattie. They told me not to be worried, but a man—"

"Yes. Mattie. Thanks for calling," Sarah broke in. Mattie could already hear the strain in Sarah's voice. "He came by here too. Can I come over?"

"Sure. Please do . . . You okay?"

"Yeah, I'll be okay. I'll be right over. Thanks, Mattie."

Mattie liked Sarah immensely. With Gus and Charlie being so close, Mattie and Sarah had, likewise, cultured and maintained a close friendship over the years. Unconsciously, she and Gus had assumed an almost parent-like role in the relationship, although their respective ages weren't disparate enough to warrant it. Mattie was always hinting that she thought Sarah and the Kid should make their relationship official. Sarah always countered with "Why ruin a perfectly good relationship?" To Sarah, she and Charlie were simply best friends.

The two sat up most of the night, deciding they would embark on the three-hour drive to Mica's place in the morning. Neither knew exactly where the place was; but they'd simply call Lieutenant Dolt, or whatever his name was, with the State Troopers.

At about the same time as Mattie and Sarah were trying to calm each other's nerves and planning the drive, I awoke from a nightmare-filled sleep. The pain in my legs was excruciating. A million thick dull needles were probing every skin pore, trying to gain painful entry into my swollen feet. Terrified of examining the damage done by the combination of frost and the abuse of the dark trail, I nonetheless unzipped the bag and looked. The catatonic sleep, which had lasted nearly twenty hours, had been sufficient time to thaw the frozen outer tissues, allowing blood to once again begin flowing to my extremities. The swelling had subsided somewhat, and my right ankle and most of the foot looked almost normal. The toes, though, had turned gray and had what looked like wet white tissue paper bubbled up and peeling off. Pus oozed from various places between the toes. My left foot, fortunately, appeared better, although it was still puffy and sore. The repulsive sight of my toes made me shudder and gag, eventually to the point of unavoidable, violent vomiting. The horror I'd witnessed, I suspect, and the racing mind that followed, resulted in another few hours of unconscious sleep.

Awakening hours later, again wracked by pain and panic, terribly thirsty, and with a noticeable fever, I, at least, was able to think somewhat more clearly. It was absolutely black inside the tent, and there appeared to be not a whisper of wind. I arranged the stove inside the tent and soon was able to scrape enough snow from outside the tent entrance to fill the tiny aluminum pot and melt it down for soup. Virtually the entire night was spent alternately dozing, drinking, and eating. Eating voraciously. Frantically. I couldn't get enough liquids and food to satisfy my cravings. I took this as a good sign, and with the fever seeming to subside, my general outlook raised a bit. I wasn't ready to give up yet, a considerably different outlook than I'd had several hours earlier. Mica would return in a couple of days, and I could last that long.

The relative calm of the previous night's weather hadn't changed much by dawn. No wind was there to chill me. Clouds still shrouded the mountains but had lifted considerably. No more rain or snow was falling, and the temperature seemed to have moderated. After examining my miserable feet again, I had unzipped the tent and found the once-complete snow cover to have diminished, melted off in the warming temperatures to the point of covering only about 50 percent of the ground.

I was angry at myself for what had happened following Gus's ill-fated fall. My inability to cope with the mental trauma had resulted in serious repercussions to my physical well-being. The shock and grief of Gus's death had dictated my actions for the past two days, and I resolutely decided that Gus deserved more respect than to be just left to stiffen on the rocks. Mental pictures developed of bears and wolverines disemboweling and dismembering the corpse. Ravens were fighting over the right to pluck out his eyes and shit on his chest. I had to return and retrieve him. Get him wrapped up and down to the landing site on the glacier so Mica and I could respectfully return him to town and prepare him for a proper burial.

By late morning, I had made the decision to return up the drainage, no matter what amount of pain it would cost. I owed Gus at least that much. I found, however, that my boots were now several sizes too small to contain my swollen feet. I'd brought a pair of beat-up Nike's that I wore as camp shoes, and they'd have to do. After another reasonably heavy meal and a half-dozen aspirin, I grunted and moaned and was able to get into the sneakers. I assembled what gear I thought I'd need for the day, including Gus's sleeping bag, a bit of food, and the small campstove. With the idea of fashioning a ladder-like travois, I cut the two longest and stoutest willows I could find near camp; and, though certainly painful to my feet, I headed back up the bottom of the drainage. Each step was excruciating, but as the trek continued, the renewed activity and the aspirin combined to diminish the apparent pain.

I knew it couldn't be more than two miles, but the journey seemed endless. The last couple hundred yards up the mountain toward Gus's body was the worst. The shoes were woefully inadequate for supporting my ankles, and I could feel the increased abrasion against the dead tissue on my toes. I was relieved to see, from a distance, that the scavengers hadn't descended on the site. The patchy snow was largely undisturbed, even around the two abandoned pack frames containing the shrouded sheep carcass.

The snow had melted from Gus's face. His clothes were darkly stained with his blood. The haunting pasty-white skin of his face and hands was unnerving, almost sickening. I momentarily forgot my pain and frantically covered Gus's face with my jacket. I couldn't bear to look at the lifeless form. Despair and a sense of defeat came over me again, as I sat down, trying to regain some trace of composure.

I tied Gus's pack frame to the long poles and was finally able to get his now-stiff body into the sleeping bag and lashed onto the poles. They weren't long enough to keep his boot heels from dragging, but I'd done the best I could with the limited resources at hand. Getting off the mountain to the bottom was, once more, frustrating and difficult; and I'd dropped the travois ends several times, refusing to watch as the tied bundle rolled and thudded off the rocks. My strength wasn't there, and I cursed myself for the treatment the corpse was receiving.

We finally arrived at the creek, which was now swollen and dirty with the recent snow melt. I too was swollen and dirty. Gus was too, undoubtedly, but at least beyond caring. After a much-needed break for black tea, thick soup, and handfuls of raisins, nuts, and chocolate, we stumbled and jolted down toward camp. My watch showed the date as September 18, and I knew Mica was only a day or two away.

Arriving back at the spike camp, the inevitable deepening shadows preceding darkness had descended. I was able to start a small fire and inspect the day's damage inflicted on my feet. The left was none the worse for wear, actually feeling reasonably well. The right, however, with the frostbitten toes, was grim. Blood and pus had oozed throughout the day, soaking my socks and toe of my shoe. The normally simple task of peeling off my sock was impossible. I heated water in the small pot and repeatedly dripped clean tepid water on my foot from the instep to the toes. Although I knew I'd need some at a later point, I swallowed the remaining half-dozen aspirin and peeled and cut away the sock. The process took at least a half hour; and I was soaked with cold sweat, shaking with pain, by the time I'd removed the sock and cleaned the angry mass. The smell of rotting flesh, the sight of the tissue damage, and the unbearable pain were overwhelming. I considered a tourniquet, something to restrict the blood from circulating the rot through my body, infecting other extremities and organs. There would probably be drastic and irreversible consequences, but it would need to be done. The stress of the day, though, put off my decision; and I again slumped into a fitful, nightmarish semisleep.

Activity at the Glacier Lodge was beginning to wane. Since the military was unable to locate any trace of a distress signal with their sophisticated aerial monitoring of thousands of square miles, they had discontinued the search. The previous days' search again failed to turn up anything positive; thus, the official search was winding down. After all, it was pointed out, this was Alaska, where the per capita number of private pilots was the highest in the world. This was also September, a time when even the most novice pilots all considered themselves the best bush pilots around; and they, practically daily, were turning up missing in the vast wilderness, or wrecked and disabled on remote hunting strips all over the state. Other searches had to be instigated.

With the skeleton crew assembled around the lodge headquarters, some serious questions needed to be asked. Answers were needed. Don, the specialist from the rescue coordination center in Anchorage, had assembled Tom, Pop, Lonny, and Alex Thomas, the remaining Alaska State Trooper.

"Some of these questions are insensitive, but at this point, I've got to ask them," he started. "I don't like asking them, especially in this situation where I have known Mica for years. You guys know him better, and I need honest answers.

"First, we've got to look at the possible angles. Is there a possibility that Mica disappeared purposefully? Was he avoiding something? Were there taxes or other debts that he'd just as soon get away from, enough to stage an accident, with him now sitting comfortably in Mexico or some other place?" Don had carefully chosen his words in an attempt to not anger Mica's friends. His eyes roved the small aggregation of pilots, and he received adamantly shaking heads in reply.

Pop was the only one to speak. "That ain't a possibility . . . next question." He said it flatly, a noticeable angry inflection in his reply.

"Although we've reviewed his flight medical examination record, did any of you know of any medical reason he shouldn't have been flying? Heart murmurs, recent headaches or blackouts, alcohol consumption, anything like that?"

Again, Pop responded for them all. "No. Absolutely not . . . Next question."

"Could they have gone a completely different direction, and we're looking in the wrong place?"

Pop continued as spokesman for the group. "I don't think so, Don. These two guys were sheep hunters. Sheep populations are down in the Talkeetna Mountains, and I doubt seriously if they'd have gone there. The only other option for sheep is in the Wrangells, and you've got to be a local resident to hunt there. The Feds have all that country tied up in Park, so they wouldn't go there. The Alaska Range is too far. I got no doubt they headed for the Chugach Range, but there's a lotta ground to cover there, as you've seen in the past few days."

"I agree," Tom put in. "It's sure possible that the weather held them out of the Matanuska, so I say we continue looking to the east. We can't just write him off."

"I'm not saying we've got to quit, but we're running out of options," Don replied.

After a pause, he continued, "At this point, I think it's safe to assume there's been an accident. We need to make an educated guess as to the probability of that accident being before or after Mica dropped off the two hunters."

"I don't like to admit there was a crash, but I guess I gotta face reality," Pop said. "It's just been too damn long, and the weather hasn't been unflyable for an entire week now. If weather had him holed up somewhere, he'd have had plenty of chances to come back by now. Tom, we didn't see any indication that anybody'd been to Futility Strip for better than a week when you and I stopped there the other day. My bet is, Don, that they either didn't make it that far, or Mica dropped them off in some other location."

"Yeah, they hadn't been to Futility," Tom addressed the group. "I'd agree with your guess there, Pop. If we assume they didn't all go down together, we gotta be looking real close, not only for a downed airplane, but for two hunters as well."

"Do any of you guys know these two hunters?" Don continued his questioning. "Are they green first timers, or have they got experience in the hills?"

"Anna, Mica's daughter, says they've been hunting this country with Mica off and on for years," Tom answered. "I remember meeting them both with Mica several years ago. I'd assume they're probably pretty skookum in the hills."

"Okay," Don continued, "unless any of you have objections, I say we still concentrate on searching for the airplane. Two experienced sheep hunters will find a way to get somebody's attention when they aren't picked up within a day or two of the appointed time. Meanwhile, keep an eye out for them while we're looking for Mica."

Mattie and Sarah had had no trouble following the directions to the Glacier Lodge. When they arrived around midday, the place was virtually deserted. There they managed to get directions to Mica's homestead from the lodge owner and had driven there. Although Anna was as concerned as the other two women, she gladly, gratefully, invited them to stay at the house with her if they wanted. Anna, ironically because of her young age in relation to the two older women, turned out to be the calming influence the other two needed. Even with the palpable tension of the situation, the three developed an immediate closeness. Each needed the support afforded by the others. Together they prepared lunches for the pilots to take with them and hearty home-cooked dinners each evening. Their nights, always lasting well into the morning hours, were spent in close-knit, supportive discussions about the country, themselves, and their missing loved ones.

The stress and physical strains I'd endured the day before were haunting me. I slept fitfully. Painfully. My left foot was again raw and sore where the rocks and snow had bombarded it through the light tennis shoe at every step. My shoulders were sore and red where ends of the travois poles had continuously rubbed and pounded. My right foot, now obviously dead and starting to decay, was an angry mass of blood and pus. The toes, mercifully, no longer sent unbearable pains shooting up my leg. Instead, a pounding ache emanated at the site of the tourniquet I'd applied just above the ankle. In Gus's pack, I'd found another small first aid kit he'd put together over the years and, in it, found a few codeine capsules, additional aspirin, a small bottle of penicillin tablets, and various threads, two needles, and gauze wraps. Too bad, I thought dejectedly, there was nothing there that would make him better. I swallowed an assortment of the various medications.

I knew I had to get back to the glacier, where I'd be easier to spot when Mica returned. I first thought I had to get Gus's body to the landing site but realized that I could no longer handle that task. I knew that in a day or two, Mica would return; and at that point, I had to get to a hospital or risk losing my leg. When I resolved this, I was ready to strike out, continuing down the drainage, to the glacier below.

I found I was able to get a boot on my left foot, although it was painfully tight. On my right, however, it was still impossible. I cut the upper six inches of leather off the boot. I also carved away the leather on the toe of the boot, leaving the sole on the bottom, but with nothing covering my toes. By loosening the laces and forcing the boot open as far as it would go, I was able to get it over my foot, and I could still loosen the tourniquet periodically to allow a slight blood flow. With that task completed, I began taking stock of what we had around the camp, packing what I thought was absolutely essential for the next two days. My sleeping bag was hastily stuffed into its sack, and the small tent was disassembled and rolled. I went through Gus's gear and found additional matches and a lighter, along with additional socks. The small stove, as well as enough freeze-dried food to last at least three days, was also jammed in my pack. I still had my rifle, as well as the original ten rounds of ammunition I'd brought along on the trip.

I cut willows and stacked them around and on top of Gus's body, putting rocks on top of them to keep the winds and the ravens from gaining easy entry. I knew it wouldn't deter grizzlies but justified the inadequate action by assuming that the smell of humans was something bears in this country would just as soon avoid. It was midafternoon before I was ready to continue my trek down the small valley to the glacier below.

Shouldering the pack, I realized immediately that if I was to make any reasonable progress, I couldn't proceed without a crutch. My right foot was, for all practical purposes, nothing more than a stump to hold my boot from falling off. I put down my rifle and backpack and found a workable forked willow that I could fashion into a makeshift crutch. With another hour lost, I finally departed down the boulder-strewn creek bed, refusing to look back at the out-of-place mound that interred the cold body of my lifelong companion.

That same afternoon, on the north shore of Tazlina Lake, Johnny Galbraith bent down and picked up a baseball cap that the choppy waves had deposited on the beach. From his small trapping cabin near the outlet of the lake, he was scouting the countryside for fur sign. Trapping season was still a couple of months away; but he liked to get out early and assess the area for tracks and other sign of marten, wolf, wolverine, mink, otter, beaver, and lynx that he would be trapping and snaring throughout the winter. He thought it odd to find evidence of humans along "his" lake but knew that fishermen had recently discovered the small run of king salmon that spawned in tributaries coming into the lake. With float-equipped planes, they'd descend on the lake during July and August, spoiling the pristine beauty of Johnny's surroundings. Now they were even littering the area with hats. *Next it'd be beer cans,* he thought. He thought nothing more of the cap; but since it was still in good shape, he shook the water off it, slapped it against his pant leg a couple of times, and put it on. He was pleased to find it even fit him, without having to adjust the strap in the back.

The following afternoon, Johnny sliced his canoe effortlessly through the calm waters of the lake, checking out the fur sign near where the Nelchina River entered the lake. Again, an object that didn't belong on the shoreline caught his eye, and he paddled over to it. Some sort of a seat cushion. With the same disappointment in mankind's propensity to carelessly litter his surroundings, he retrieved the cushion, throwing it in the bottom of the canoe. It was worn and water soaked, but he thought maybe when it dried out, it'd be nice to sit on in the canoe. He went about his business of the day, returning the ten miles that night along the north shore of the lake to his tiny spruce-log cabin.

Tom broke the news of the discontinuation of the official search to Anna, Mattie, and Sarah. "I don't like it either, Anna, but we're not finding any evidence of Mica or any of them. Just because the official search is over doesn't mean that I'm quitting." Mattie and Sarah stood in the driveway, openmouthed, but Anna's pent-up frustrations came out with a vengeance.

"Those mealy-mouthed, slack-jawed suits from Anchorage can just go back to their damned offices. I'll pay anyone able to fly whatever it takes to keep this thing going. I'll mortgage this miserable place, sell all the airplanes, anything to pay for continuing the search. They're not dead, Tom," she broke down, continuing between the tears and the sobs that had gripped her. "Dad's out there, Tom. You gotta find him . . ."

"Pop and I'll keep looking. Jack Osborne says he's got all his hunters out of the field now too, so he'll be helping. Lonny's got a bunch of hunters to pick up now that the seasons are over, so he's out for a while. My brother'll take care of hunters I got out. It'll be three good pairs of eyes looking. We'll keep searching."

With tears streaking her cheeks and Mattie and Sarah dejectedly following, Anna turned and, with shoulders noticeably shaking at each sob that overtook her, walked back to the house.

I wondered where the hell Mica was. It was the twenty-first of September, the day we were scheduled to be picked up. I'd made it back to the glacier and set up the tent in the same location Gus and I had made the first night's camp. It seemed like months ago that I'd listened to his banter and tasted his biscuits. I'd never have them again. Never listen to Gus's down-home advice about the universe or appreciate the one-of-a-kind campfire wit of his. Never take another hunting trip with him. He loved the mountains. Loved life. It seemed such a loss. I already missed him terribly.

Physically incapable of contending with the excruciating pain from my dead foot and mentally unwilling to contend with the anguish of Gus's death, my forces abandoned me. The next two days were little more than a blur of pain and delirium. I awoke from nightmare-filled unconsciousness at irregular intervals, soaked with sweat, urine, and putrid pus from the rotting foot. I was only able to maintain fluids by drinking huge quantities of water collected from various pots and cups set just outside the tent that were filled almost continuously by rain and drizzle running off the tent fly.

When the delirium subsided and the tangible pain returned, my wristwatch indicated the date as the twenty-fourth of September. Among myriad defeatist thoughts, I knew I must do what had been in the back of my mind for a week. My foot was dead, and with it constantly pumping poison throughout the rest of my body, it must be removed if I was to have any reasonable chance of survival. Gus was gone. Mica was not going to ride in on his white stallion and save my miserable carcass. I had to think and act for myself.

The blackness in my foot and the bleakness of the situation manifested itself in the form of a resolve to stay alive. It was doubtful, without quick transportation to a hospital, that life was maintainable for much longer. What the hell had I done? Doom was written everywhere.

The knife blade was shaking, reflecting the quivering light to various parts of the tent. The stove put out a hissing blue flame that turned yellow as it enveloped the blade, turning it black with soot, before lending a slight red glow to the steel. It would, I hoped, be enough to sterilize the blade and at the same time cauterize small vessels. Feeling was gone in my foot, but above my knee, the pain was excruciating. I laid the hot blade on my shin, just below the knee. The hair curled from the heat of the blade and put off a sickening pungent odor. At least I couldn't feel it when the blade cut through the skin and into the muscle. The tourniquet, now positioned just above my knee, was sufficient to reduce the flow of blood as I cut.

I had no recollection of the remainder of the grim operation. The survival instinct had taken over and allowed continuation. I simply don't remember the disarticulation of my lower leg at the knee, but the sickening, bloody job was completed. Sweat, blood, urine, and clear jellylike pus were smeared everywhere when I awoke from my unconscious stupor. It was dark, but my now-dim flashlight revealed only a crimson mass of clothing I'd obviously tied around the stump before I'd passed out. The flow of blood appeared to be minimal, but there was so much of it from the operation, I had a hard time telling for sure. I remembered little of what transpired, until the weak flashlight beam panned across the lifeless, surreal, red-smeared leg lying just outside the tent entrance. Feverish despair once again shrouded my world, and all went blank.

Another three days had passed, and despite relatively good weather, Tom and the other pilots still involved in the search had found nothing. The military aircraft had returned from two successful search and rescue missions farther north and had spent an additional day over the Chugach Range listening, without success, for emergency beacon signals. Satellite coverage of the area continued but had revealed nothing.

Disappointed and physically drained following another fruitless day of searching, Tom droned his SuperCub along the eastern margin of Tazlina Lake on his way from the mountains back to Mica's homestead. As he passed near the outlet of the massive glacial lake, he noticed a wisp of smoke rising from Johnny Galbraith's cabin. The lake's waters had receded somewhat, and there was ample room to settle the Cub onto the exposed sandy beach of the north shore. Within a hundred yards of the cabin, he swung the plane's nose into the gentle breeze and stopped the propeller. As he unfolded himself from the plane, he saw the welcoming grin and wave of Johnny's arm, as he walked unhurried down the path from his cabin. The wiry little Athabascan trapper seemed ageless in the waning evening light.

"Good to see you again, Johnny," Tom said as they shook hands.

"You too, buddy. What you doing here? I seen you almost ever' day flying over, but I figure you got too much money to make to stop an' see me."

"I've been busy, Johnny. I guess you've heard that Mica's been missing for a couple weeks now, and we're still looking for any sign of him."

"No." Johnny was surprised. "I ain't heard. I been out here a month now, an' I don't get too much visitors. Boy, never thought that guy would get lost. He been helpin' me out for lotta years. Boy, never thought he'd have no problems. Boy."

Tom accompanied Johnny up the short path to his cabin, and between disjointed discussions about fur prices and Mica's disappearance, he downed a quick cup of coffee before heading back to the airplane.

"If you happen to come across anything in your travels, Johnny, I'll try to stop by with groceries in a week or so. Keep your eyes open for any sign of the airplane," Tom said before hopping back into the Cub.

As Tom was about to hit the starter button and head back home, Johnny, with a serious, somewhat troubled look on his face, said, "I found something a couple days ago. It probably ain't nothin' though."

"What you got, Johnny? At this point, we need any lead we can get."

"Well, up by the Nelchina River inlet, I found a hat and a pad to sit on."

"What do you mean 'a pad'?"

"Well, boy! Something like a chair pad from a boat or a plane. I got it there in the canoe if you want it."

"Yeah, sure," Tom replied. "It might mean something."

Johnny hurried to the overturned canoe a few yards away and returned with a light green cushion. Tom didn't recognize it but at the time couldn't remember what color the cushions were in Mica's one-eighty. "Thanks, Johnny, I'll check it with Anna and bring it back out to you next week."

"Maybe you better take this hat too," he said, pulling the ball cap off his head and tossing it on the cushion in the back of the little SuperCub. "I found it along the lake pretty close to that pad."

"Thanks again, Johnny. I'll get this stuff back to you next week." Darkness was creeping in quickly, and Tom wanted to be on his way. "Is there anything else you might need before freeze-up?"

"Nope. Boy, I'm way too old for a wife and way too broke for a girlfriend. See ya later."

In less than thirty minutes, Tom was taxiing his airplane up to the gas pumps at Mica's place. As she had done every evening for the past several days, Anna came hurrying out to meet him. She and Tom embraced in the quiet half-light that remained, and for a while, no words were exchanged.

Tom finally broke the silence. "Nothing. Not a damn thing. I touched bases with Pop and Osborne on the radio this evening, and they struck out today too. Did you hear any word from the Feds about ELT hits?"

"No . . . nothing."

"I stopped at Johnny Galbraith's place down on Tazlina Lake tonight, and he had a couple things I want you to look at. They're here in the plane." Tom walked the few paces to the open Cub doors and grabbed the cushion and the hat.

Anna took the cushion and glanced at it, turning it over in her hands. "Let's take them in the house to look at them in the light," she said then added, "Dad's been wearing that old ratty blue hat lately. I doubt if he even owns one in as good of shape as that one," nodding at the cap Tom still held in his hand.

"Just a minute, Anna," Tom said. "Let's take 'em into the hangar and look before we barge into the house in front of Mattie and Sarah. They don't need to be drawn into this any sooner than need be." Tom realized the moment he said it that Anna would catch his drift, but it was too late to take back his words.

"What are you saying, Tom? Where the hell did Johnny find these? Were they in the lake?" Anna's voice cracked at the last question, and her accusing look shot at Tom like a bullet. Before Tom could answer, she continued, "Those two in the house are in this as deep as I am, Tom, and they've got a right to know what's happening. We're going in the house."

All Tom could do was follow, at once hopeful that some sign of the downed plane had been found, and equally concerned about what the location of the articles probably meant.

Anna burst through the door into the glaring light of the house. She immediately recognized the cushion as one her mother had recovered many years ago for the Cessna one-eighty. "There's no question that this came from Dad's plane . . . Was it in the lake?"

"Johnny found it washed up on the north shore. This hat was there too," Tom said as he offered the hat up for closer inspection.

Sarah, who'd been shocked by Anna's explosive entry into the house, just stared openmouthed at the hat. It was camouflaged fabric, with a circular patch sewn to the front advertising a local taxidermist shop. She recognized it immediately. She'd even worn it on occasion. There was no mistaking. All four of them understood immediately the significance of Johnny's find.

The Alaska State Troopers, following their official inquiry, reported to the families and then to the media that the aircraft piloted by Mica M. Meyers, with passengers Augustus L. Harms and Charles Lander, was assumed to have crashed into Tazlina Lake on the afternoon of September 11, 1986. It was further reported that the hull of the aircraft probably remained intact; and the occupants, if they survived the initial impact, were unable to exit the aircraft and were entombed in a watery grave beneath the glacial waters of Tazlina Lake. Freeze-up was imminent, and further efforts to locate the wreckage and the bodies would have to wait until the following summer.

The assumptions made by the Troopers were largely correct. Mica had, in fact, encountered severe turbulence on his return trip. Flying low down the glacier, a violent and unexpected wind shear had inverted the small plane, and recovery was impossible at the low altitude. The one-eighty had plowed into the frigid waters, killing Mica on impact; and the plane, unseen and unheard by humans, had quickly vanished beneath the wind-whipped surface. The lake was hundreds of feet deep. No emergency locator beacon could send a reasonable signal through hundreds of feet of silty glacial water. The fact that my hat was found, however, resulted in a disastrously incorrect assumption.

SURVIVAL

The instinct to survive had, fortunately, overridden my queasiness and terrible pain. Various accounts have shown the human body capable of overcoming tremendous insult and adversity if that survival instinct is strong. In dealing with the events of the past two weeks, it was obvious that that innate quest for survival had been marginally sufficient. That, however, was with a healthy and fit body; and perhaps more importantly, it was while there was still hope. Would the mental blow to the psyche prove to be the knockout punch?

Every day, indeed, every hour, would now constitute a physical and mental test of my endurance in an environment as harsh as can be imagined. Nature must be contended with, not in terms that nature writers and poets usually recreate in their writings, but on a scale that is dramatically unforgiving and relentless. During the best of seasons, she is able to mete out punishment that will instantly kill the strongest willed and the most physically able. When less-than-ideal conditions persist, she can provide the basis for nothing less than a morbid nightmare. Forgiveness is not an attribute that is commonly dispensed.

I tried to logically arrange my predicament and, further, to formulate workable plans. My partner was dead. I was crippled. Mica wasn't coming back.

What were my options, in this gray time of year when winter's onset was imminent? Survival experts will expound on the virtues of staying put. They profess that someone will always come along and find you. They're undoubtedly correct, but I was lucid enough to know that to be found five years later as a pile of bleached bones and a few strands of raven-picked sinew by some wayward sheep hunter was not my idea of a positive outcome.

Where was Mica? Why were there no squadrons of airplanes constantly droning beneath the low-lying clouds in search of me? Surely the weather conditions here were worse than lower down, and even here, there had been days when flying conditions were reasonable. Had some catastrophe occurred? An event like nuclear holocaust? What the hell had gone so terribly wrong?

In the mountains, the tremendous snowpack and the temperature extremes that were always compounded by relentless winds resulted in a less-than-inviting scenario. I decided that, although travel would be agonizingly slow, I needed to descend to lower country, where I could at least gather enough firewood to melt snow for water, cook my meager but life-sustaining meals, and maintain warmth. Perhaps my sluggish trail in the snow would be noticed by a searching pilot, and I would finally be plucked from these tortuous mountains.

Two days of rest proved to be a double-edged sword. On one hand, my fever had finally ebbed, and I'd had a chance to gain a small but decisive victory over the constant ooze of blood and pus from what remained of my leg. On the other hand, food supplies had continued to dwindle; and even more disconcerting, the mental gymnastics ongoing in my mind were not leading me toward a healthy outlook on life.

The weather was brutal, never constant for more than a few hours at a time. The changeover to winter meant a redirection of the flow patterns of upper air masses, bringing moisture-laden clouds up from the Gulf of Alaska, dumping enormous loads of snow, rain, or sleet as they topped over the mighty Chugach Range.

Largely because of that ever-changing weather, I found I was developing a daily routine that allowed recuperation. Sleep was interrupted frequently either by wind gusts that would flap at the tent fly or because of an uncomfortable oozing of putrefaction from my stump. Often, condensation would accumulate on the roof of the tent in large-enough quantities to coalesce into an icy droplet that would invariably target my exposed face or neck. Sleep, thus frequently interrupted, still consumed probably eighteen hours of every twenty-four. Cooking, eating, and cleansing of wounds combined to use up the remainder of the day.

On about the fifth day of this extended layover, I gimped out of the tent on my makeshift crutch to rid my bowels of some freeze-dried macaroni and sheep meat effluent. The world was white. Glimpsed through the half-light of dusk, the stark black cliffs that were too steep to provide an adequate foothold for the day's accumulation of snow looked eerie. Only about fifty yards away, however, was a smaller dark form that contrasted dramatically with the blank background.

The falling snow relented for a half breath, allowing mutual attention. I recognized the sow grizzly from my earlier encounter some two weeks previously. This real estate, with its jumbled moraines, adequate water, and general lack of human influence, was obviously her home. My presence, although outwardly unaggressive, undoubtedly caused concern. The bear herself seemed only a bit curious, if not indifferent.

I retreated cautiously back to the tent, gaining an altogether false sense of security upon entering the confines of the flimsy nylon dome. Before zipping the door closed, I peered back in the direction of the bear. It too had approached the tent and was no more than forty yards from me. Although appearing unrealistically large against the snowy background, she didn't give me the impression that she was a threat.

At that distance, even through the falling snow and the dwindling light, I was afforded a clear view, able to discern even minute details. When the grizz turned her head sideways, looking down the glacier, I could easily see she was carrying something in her massive jaws. When I realized what it was she had, a deep, animalistic, surging anger welled up immediately. I screamed insanely, primordially, trying to run at her. In retrospect, it was fortunate that I immediately stumbled, falling facedown in the wet snow not more than five yards from the base of the tent. My anger doubled; and I screamed again in mixed pain, anguish, and frustration. I crawled half into the tent, frantically groping for my rifle in the leaden darkness. By the time I'd pulled the gun from its hiding place beneath scattered clothing, the bear had vanished. I was left sitting in the snow, panting and soaked. I was shaking uncontrollably, not from the cold, not from fear, nor from the physical exertion. It was the sick, gruesome image that was burned forever into my memory. The grizzly had been carrying the lower half of a human leg.

I was another two days readying for my departure. Sleep was now elusive, as horror-filled dreams recurred within minutes of falling asleep. Even in those nightmares, however, the bear remained unaggressive. She simply stared at me stupidly, a portion of the white leg protruding from either side of her snout, saliva dripping from the toes on one side. I assumed the leg was what was left of my own. Possibly it was from Gus's tomb. It didn't really matter; but I tried, usually unsuccessfully, to rid this haunting vision from my memory.

I had always considered myself to be far from squeamish. After all, I'd just "buried" my best friend after having him die in my arms. I'd somehow managed to excise my own leg and sew the skin tight over the stump with some thread from Gus's sewing kit. But for some reason, the idea of a grizzly sow gnawing on a human extremity, sharing tidbits with her offspring, grating teeth against the bones, licking at the marrow, was offending and repulsive.

Even with my diminished appetite, the food reserves were dwindling rapidly. Winter can be a hungry time in interior Alaska, and I knew I'd need to either supplement my meager supply, conserve what little I had, or count on being rescued soon. I made the logical decision to do all three, knowing that the last "course of action" was largely out of my control.

The threat to my continued existence on this earth increased with each new snowfall. Time was clearly the enemy. The likelihood of a major storm increased exponentially every day, as did the chances of the temperatures declining precipitously. Both of these impending weather factors had to be contended with. Of the options I had available, the best course of action was to get the hell out of the mountains.

Obviously, I'd need to travel light. Food, shelter, and a firearm were essential; most other accouterments must be abandoned. Most of one day was spent fashioning a serviceable and somewhat comfortable crutch. With two good legs and dry ground, the traveling in this terrain was sometimes difficult. With one leg and a mantle of snow to camouflage the footholds, it would be horrendous. The lighter I could travel, the better.

On the morning of the third day of October, I departed. I hadn't seen or heard an aircraft for at least ten days; and I suspected, rather gloomily, it would be another ten months before humans had reason to invade these mountains again for another August sheep hunting season. Fortunately, the snow had been relatively light. About eight inches of fluffy, light snow had accumulated atop a two- or three-inch base of once wet, now crusted, snow. I recalled a February drive through Thompson Pass, not more than fifty miles from this very location, when the snow had piled up to well over twenty feet. Would it be much different here in a couple of months?

Frustrations were many, progress little. Simply the amount of time it now took me to complete the simplest tasks was disheartening. How much time does the average outdoorsman ponder the simple, but necessary, act of expelling bodily wastes? Perhaps the neophyte will experiment with various postures before becoming comfortable without a porcelain throne upon which to nestle. It had never crossed my mind how such a simple and mundane act as squatting beside a boulder could become a messy affair. When you've only got one leg, believe me, it ain't as simple a process as it sounds. I was having to relearn how to be a human.

As my strength returned following the amputation and subsequent sickness, my mind wandered, taking trips back in time to more pleasurable occasions. Sarah occupied most of my daydreams. I found I frequently became angry with myself when I thought about her struggling through every day and every night. *Had she written me off, as all the others apparently had?* I couldn't believe they'd just leave me out here to contend with whatever was dealt. No. Sarah and Mattie would never give up on Gus and me. I made another mental note, for the umpteenth time, to leave an unmistakable trail in the snow should the search planes return.

Food was becoming a real problem. I scavenged the little black crowberries when I could find them. At one point, I sacrificed one of my few, precious rifle cartridges for a half-pound ptarmigan. Remaining rations consisted of a few dried fruits, ground coffee and a half-dozen tea bags, a few small packages of dried noodles, a fistful of rice, ten candy bars, a couple tablespoons of sugar, and, fortunately, about three pounds of salt. Although the salt was burdensome, it was always a staple on our hunting trips, normally used for preserving capes and pelts of harvested animals. I was thankful again for Gus's insistence on always bringing the salt.

Progress was excruciatingly slow. By the time I was finally packed and ready to go, that first day amounted to only a few short, grueling, hours. The adjacent glacier, I was sure, was moving down the mountain at a pace greater than my own. Maybe it would be quicker if I just set up camp on the ice and let it slowly carry me northward. My crutch, fashioned from an ancient and gnarled willow, was adequate but, at the same time, quite cumbersome. Though padded with a piece of Gus's sleeping pad, it nonetheless chafed and irritated my armpit. Hobbling along through snow-covered, boulder-strewn glacial effluent that first afternoon resulted in countless falls. Countless bruises. Countless aches. But by far the most defeating and disheartening aspect was the lack of noticeable progress. As I began erecting my tent in which to sleep off the day's exertion, I could look back up the valley not more than a half mile, less than a thousand yards, and plainly pick out my previous campsite. Once again, to traverse only this minuscule distance resulted in a mental blow that was truly devastating when I considered what I'd been through in that first long day, comparing it with the grueling days, maybe weeks, maybe even months, that lay ahead.

Physical exhaustion, armpit blisters, and a ravenous appetite were the only rewards. Against my better judgment, I consumed twice the amount of food I'd rationed myself for the day. Even eating only the stingy portions I'd allotted myself resulted in a larder that was now woefully meager. Unless I supplemented the grub, it would be gone in a matter of days.

On October 12, as had become habit over the last several days, I was again readying myself and what few belongings I had for the day's march, when I was presented with an opportunity to increase the size of my larder. The small band of ewes and their lambs presented somewhat of a quandary, however. I certainly needed the protein, and opportunities like this would probably diminish substantially as I continued my trek down the glacier. However, killing one of the sheep would invariably mean an additional day or two before I could resume moving; and when I did continue, it would be with additional weight. The tempting thought of fresh sheep meat was more than I could resist, and I came up with the only realistic compromise I could imagine.

As the small band grazed down the windswept hillside not more than a hundred yards from me, I decided to expend another precious cartridge to tip over a lamb. I waited as motionless as I could for close to an hour before they had moved onto the jumbled moraine. When the opportunity for a clean broadside shot presented itself, the rifle bucked, and the small lamb was down. The remaining eight sheep clambered back up the scree in seconds, quickly disappearing among the boulders and snowfields above me.

The lamb meat was a godsend. Probably not more than forty pounds live, it provided four meals over the next two days, with a few pounds of smoke- and salt-dried strips for a few days to come. A piece of the belly skin was ideal for wrapping the top of my crutch, providing more comfortable padding than the foam I'd been using.

By the light of the small flickering campfire that night, I began reflecting on my predicament, and the precarious hold I had on life itself. In just a month's time, I'd gone from being a recreational sportsman, back through eons, to more basic, primordial roots. Simple survival was the overriding force that dictated every action. All activities were necessarily calculated to best serve that goal of surviving. My lackadaisical attitude toward life had been modified immensely. Everything I did was with but a single purpose: to survive.

Even my appearance had changed dramatically. Of course, the lack of half of one leg was outwardly obvious. Whiskers covered most of my face, and those surfaces left exposed had become sun- and wind-burned leather. There was a new leanness and tautness in my body I hadn't before been able to attain.

With all the outward physical changes, however, probably the most profound change was within, perhaps only noticeable in attitude, demeanor, or through the new, somewhat haunted look in my eyes. Hardships build character, I've been told. If these physical and emotional hardships are less than it takes to kill me, I suspect I'll be one hell of a character when I emerge from the wilderness back into my former life. I'd lost my partner and best friend. I'd lost a leg. I'd lost at least twenty pounds of muscle and flesh. As yet, though, I had yet to lose my drive . . . my desire for life . . . my *soul.*

I resumed my trek on the third day following the killing of the sheep. Wind and falling snow combined their treacherous forces, making travel all the more dangerous. To dally longer could mean an indeterminable time before the storm let up, so I resolved to push on in spite of the grim conditions. I'd begun to measure daily distances traveled in terms of hundreds of yards rather than in miles. To hope for a mile was beyond reason. The terrain, the weather conditions, and my physical debilities dictated that I move slowly and cautiously. Combined with my constant need to search out any and all possible food sources, the amount of real estate traversed during the course of a day was minuscule.

Periodically, I'd find my trail passing through various-sized glades where short tundra vegetation had taken root. Although more often than not these areas were covered by varying amounts of snow, the footing underneath was noticeably more forgiving. Upon stumbling upon these matted tundra islands among the otherwise boulder-covered terrain, I generally lingered long enough to gather a handful or two of the scant, frozen, bitter crowberries. Whether or not the caloric intake was worth the effort was questionable, but it did provide a periodic diversion to my travels.

Another week or ten days elapsed with very few diversions from my "walk a day, rest a day" routine. All that remained of the scant rations I'd begun the trip with was a half pound or so of salt. I had consumed virtually all food except for a handful of jerked sheep meat. I appraised the remaining supplies one evening by flickering campfire. In addition to the salt and dried meat, I had thirty-three wooden matches and three partially used matchbooks, enough, if used sparingly, to last perhaps a few months. Five rifle cartridges were all that remained in my arsenal. The fuel for the small campstove was gone, so the stove itself had been abandoned a few camps back. I still had the tent, and despite the occasional winds that threatened to destroy the fiberglass poles and the fabric itself, it was marginally serviceable yet. A rifle, a lightweight sleeping bag, a change of clothes (including Gus's lightweight parka), two knives, an aluminum boiling pot and a small frying pan, and a four-inch sharpening steel were about all the additional supplies I had. I reminded myself that the utmost stinginess was no longer an option. To be otherwise at this point would be courting disaster.

Most often, at the end of a day of travel, I'd be so exhausted that I would collapse and sleep. Other times, I'd reserve enough energy to pitch my tent and take small solace in a small fire. On those nights, staring into the flickering flames, my mind invariably retreated to far easier times, usually with Sarah.

Although Sarah and I had spent the previous fifteen years together, juggling our respective professional schedules to allow mutual vacation time had been difficult. We'd trekked the Australian Outback near Alice Springs for several weeks together and had floated and fished more than a dozen river systems throughout North America. Weekends and day trips were invariably close to home.

One magical place in particular had etched such an indelible memory that my campfire daydreams continued to resurrect. An officially unnamed drainage on the north side of the Alaska Range was our mutual favorite. We'd first stumbled upon the location while on a preseason scouting trip for new sheep hunting territory. We referred to it as First Gold Creek in honor of the nugget Sarah had excitedly plucked from the streambed. We had returned on several occasions, simply to unwind. It was our spot, and like adolescents making a blood promise, we'd vowed never to take others there or divulge its exact location.

First Gold Creek drained the heart of the Alaska Range just to the west of Mount McKinley. Its headwaters were borne in a spring percolating from what appeared to be the exact center of a hanging glacial cirque. The amphitheater surrounding the cirque on three sides was composed of light granitic cliffs, perhaps five hundred feet high. The bowl itself was carpeted with lichens, mosses, and grasses, with a smattering of stunted willows alongside the creek. It was nothing less than surreal. Morning sun glowed off the cliffs. Never were there any bugs. We laughed, teased, frolicked in the early August splendor on our annual pilgrimage to First Gold. It was there that our love for each other was resolidified, where we could shed both our inhibitions and our clothes, ridding our minds of superfluous worries. To simply close my eyes and imagine Sarah's naked wanderings through the lush green carpets of First Gold Creek was enough to maintain my desire to continue living.

Although contending with the elements pushed me virtually to the limits of my physical and mental abilities on an almost daily basis, I felt that I was, for the first time, in my rightful element. Perhaps it was simply a rationalization, to cope with the almost hopeless fact that winter had set upon me. Or the fact that I was ill prepared for the upcoming weeks or months. A deep, intangible feeling overwhelmed me at times, providing an inner calm. I had no superfluous, random thoughts banging around inside. I was truly focused. To survive was my singular objective; to do so necessitated the use of every skill I had ever learned. It also would require no small amount of luck.

Up to this point in my struggles, I had convinced myself that discovery by a search party would be forthcoming. I simply needed to survive another day. Perhaps a week at the most, and the searching SuperCubs would finally come for me. Aside from the daydreams of easier times with Sarah, nights around my campfires were devoted to journal notes, planning on what I needed to do the following day, contemplating where the next meal would be coming from, and being rescued. My thoughts took me back in time to another trip several years before.

Gus and I had flown into the Innoko River country from the small Kuskokwim village of McGrath. It happened to be a year that neither of us had taken a moose. We discovered the savory fact that the Fish and Game management unit there possessed a November season for moose, which was in itself a rarity. Knowing that the weather during November is more often than not absolutely miserable, we had been dropped off by a ski plane in an area with hordes of post-rutting monster bulls. We'd arranged with the air taxi operator to pick us up eight days later, but if he happened to be in the area in two or three days, we wanted him to check on us (fat chance!). If we had a moose, we'd be ready to return.

As it turned out, the next morning Gus tipped over a beautiful bull; and with our small plastic sleds, we'd dragged the moose quarters back to our campsite. Five days passed with no sign of the airplane, and Gus got a bit restless. He rigged an ingenious signaling device, which he swore the first airplane flying within forty miles was sure to see. True to his word, the first airplane we'd seen or heard in six days was spotted the next day, and Gus lured him in like a trout on a line. His method was unique.

Gus found a mostly dead old white spruce standing more or less alone in a large clearing no more than a hundred yards from our camp. He'd climbed the tree and tied up a gallon can of white gas. At the base of the tree, he'd built and maintained a small campfire. When the passing plane was heard, then spotted, he calmly fired a couple of quick rounds from his .338 Remington into the can, veritably exploding the contents. The fuel sprayed over most of the limbs, and not a small amount washed down to the fire. Between the time he shot and the time that the tree exploded into flames was no more than ten seconds. The Roman candle effect caught the passing pilot's attention, and he landed less than five minutes later, eyes as big as a tin of Copenhagen, wondering what in hell we were up to. It served our purpose well, as we were back in the McGrath bar, hooting and hollering with the locals, by dark that evening.

Unfortunately, I was without two of the major ingredients for effecting a similar outcome. I was missing the gallon can of Blazo, and thus far, I was without any passing aircraft.

The next six days brought nothing remarkable, except, perhaps, that I was still alive. I was able to take a small bit of comfort in knowing that my tortured body was responding well to the rigors of the travel and to the meager rations. The weather continued relatively mild. Intermittent snow flurries resulted in very little new accumulation. Persistent winds in this relatively open environment deposited three feet of snow in some places while leaving others bare. This made for treacherous footing. I continued north, descending along the lateral border of the glacier. I was able to travel only every other day, with a day of rest between those days of travel. My progress seemed to increase, and by the end of October, I'd probably covered a straight-line distance of about four miles. I was glad snails were not migratory, as the sight of a herd of them passing me by would have been like the proverbial final straw on the camel's back.

The slightly lower elevation had brought an increase in the quantity and size of the vegetation. Willows became more numerous, and there was now even a sporadic stunted spruce attempting to eke out an existence in a sheltered hollow. I took notice, not because of any horticultural interest, but because it meant an easier time finding reasonable firewood. During intermittent periods when there were no clouds below me, I could now see inviting stands of taiga, the boreal interior forest. I knew that once I reached its fringes, food and shelter, meaning, literally, life, would be easier. Of greater importance was the fact that it meant being one step closer to civilization.

The word "subsistence" has a variety of meanings, depending on the person asked. All too often in Alaska, living a subsistence lifestyle means buying enough groceries in the local store to subsist between unemployment checks, food stamps, and various other governmental giveaway programs. Very few people live a lifestyle that I view as truly subsistence. It's not an easy road. Even in bush Alaska, subsistence gathering, unfortunately, is usually practiced at the local post office. I'd spent weeks and weeks in association with "subsistence" peoples of the north and was virtually always disappointed in their lack of incentive and "nondependence" on available natural resources.

Now, however, my situation was rapidly dictating that I become truly a subsistence user. My rations were extremely meager, and now, even my ammunition was limited. Every opportunity to gather sustenance from the land was taken advantage of. Berries were few, but each one encountered was plucked and savored. Mushrooms, though pitifully lacking in caloric value, were saved and boiled with the remaining dried sheep meat. I thickened broth with caribou moss and witch's hair. I shaved shelf fungus or mashed cranberries or crowberries into my tea. Nothing was inedible, and at the same time, nothing was providing the necessary nutrients for sustained health.

I'd begun to lose track of time. My watchband had apparently broken during some unremembered ordeal, and the watch had disappeared. How many days since Gus had died? How many weeks since I had seen and embraced my Sarah? My days of recuperation entailed countless hours of sleep. The rigors of the trek, combined with inadequate food and my body's need to stave off infections, must have compounded my insatiable appetite for sleep.

I decided, as one day of rest between agonizing travel developed into two days of rest, that I'd be better off exercising my mind as well. I rummaged through my clothing and found my all-weather notebook and a pencil and began, only halfheartedly, to keep a relatively lucid journal of my activities. This, I found, provided a calming and satisfying way to assess and contemplate what I was going through.

Winter began descending with a vengeance. The ever-shortening days were accompanied by declining temperatures and increasing duration of storms. Winds often became unbearable, necessitating frequent stops. If my food situation had been more reasonable, I'd have opted to throw together a semipermanent shelter and avoid the worst of the blizzards. I realized, however, that was not a viable option. I had to keep moving, however slowly and painfully, always on the lookout for food and firewood.

I found myself unable to record only the grim episodes in my journal. Despite my predicament, there were notable exceptions to the mundane task of forever pushing onward. The few clear nights, although painfully cold, were resplendent with auroras. Curtains of greens, yellows, and reds undulated in their subzero splendor. Blasts of light spread across the skies, dimming the twinkling of northern stars. I had viewed their enthralling beauty and strength countless times in years past but had never experienced the volume and depth I was treated to during these nights.

Calm days too offered up their spellbinding beauty. I staggered into a small opening in the now ever-present spruce. A fresh blanket of snow had smoothed the landscape. The only relief was a lone set of ermine tracks crisscrossing the small opening, random patterns of nonrandom footfalls in the pristine white. No one, not even the devil himself, could look upon this vast land and not see, no *feel*, the beauty.

The awesome grandeur of the landscape was a mental boost but did nothing for the physical requirements for warmth and food. The almost-daily snows effectively obliterated my tracks within hours of passing, making it virtually impossible for airborne searchers to find me. It became apparent that, if survival was possible, it depended entirely on me.

Using only guesswork in attempting to account for the lost days, the season had progressed well into November. I had descended into the Tazlina Lake country, where firewood was plentiful. Unfortunately, however, the lack of food was becoming more than a nuisance. New holes punched in my belt signaled a decreasing waist size. A gaunt face was hidden by a now-full beard, providing an ice-covered blanket of insulation throughout the long days.

I was still trying to move along the spruce-covered sidehill at the margins of the lake at least every third day. Progress, while slow enough in the beginning, was becoming more difficult because of the increasing snow depths. Ice was forming around the shallows of the lake, but not yet thick enough for travel. Nights when winds were quiet were filled with creaks, groans, and pings of newly forming ice, often lending an accompaniment to the dance of the northern lights overhead.

It was along the margins of the lake that I stumbled, quite literally, across a windfall. Hidden by the spruce a few dozen yards up from the lake, and almost wholly covered by new snow, I all but fell over a ragged and bent piece of metal tubing. Looking around a bit further, I found more twisted and sheared-off tubing, finally understanding the significance of the find. Obviously, sometime in the past twenty or thirty years, an airplane had met with major misfortune along the desolate banks. I was relieved to find no evidence of its occupants; hopefully, they'd survived and been rescued. Although I found what I thought to be the wreckage of the entire plane, the engine and most of the panel-mounted gauges had been removed. I thought of the multitude of derelict planes and miscellaneous parts I'd seen at Mica's and surmised that he'd likely been responsible for salvage of usable parts from this old bird.

One of the wings was largely intact, although crumpled and devoid of all but a ragged swatch or two of fabric. It did, however, have a piece of thin aluminum peeled back from the top. As the proverbial cartoon character with the lightbulb incandescing with a bright idea, I was enthralled by my good fortune.

It was relatively easy to unscrew the metal with my knife and flatten the few crinkles in the thin, lightweight aluminum. Hewing out some spruce branches, I was able to fashion a frame, and once the metal was attached by "sewing" with what was left of the rudder and aileron control cables, I had completed a serviceable sled. At about two feet wide and nearly six feet long, it could be towed almost effortlessly behind me, allowing a tremendous reduction in the load I'd been carrying in my backpack.

The aircraft cable, in addition to providing "thread" for splicing together the toboggan, had an additional, equally important, role. I found that I was able to reduce one cable into seven equal, smaller strands of braided wire. Each of those pieces, left in the campfire for a few minutes to de-temper, could be straightened and fashioned into an individual, small-diameter snare.

A leaning pole, unbaited, with four or five snares positioned in series up the pole, resulted in the capture of a tree squirrel during the first day. No waste of my precious few bullets and enough meat to provide a few morsels of sustenance. The possibilities of squirrel and rabbit stew loomed high in my dreams.

As long as I was mobile enough to search out squirrel middens where cone piles often as tall as I and sometimes twenty or thirty feet across the base were stored by the squirrels, my snaring efforts were fruitful. One, sometimes two, squirrels per day was enough to add significantly to my pot. A week of snaring resulted in eleven catches. I found, however, that it paid worthwhile dividends to check the snares daily.

In one case, owing to particularly nasty weather, I left the snares for two days between checks. A squirrel had obviously become ensnared during the first twenty-four hours, as it was as frozen as a drugstore popsicle when I retrieved it. Skinning while frozen, of course, was impossible. So, on the trek back to camp, I put the frozen little body under my clothes, figuring my body heat would speed the thawing process of the critter; and it would be ready to skin and consume when I arrived at the makeshift shelter. I wasn't ready for the consequences.

Rather than always departing from a cooling carcass, it seems that at least a few of the parasites must hibernate, waiting for conditions to improve. As the carcass warmed between my ragged tee shirt and my belly, the saber-toothed cooties were resurrected from their temporary torpor; and as a bear emerging from its winter hibernaculum, they were voracious. A few hundred yards from camp, I began to itch. By the time I'd arrived, I felt as though my belly button was packed with poison ivy. I must have been a sight as I realized what was transpiring. I came hobbling into my snowy camp, long greasy unkempt hair and white beard, snot-cicles dangling from my nose, emitting high-speed expletives like this country hadn't before heard, stripping off clothing as fast as I could manage.

It's easy to understand the average hunter's misconceptions concerning wildlife abundance of Alaska. Every outdoor sporting magazine on the stands gushes with pretty pictures and flowery prose about the majesty of the land, the abundance of wildlife, the magnificent success of the hunter. Videographers spend a day or two in Denali Park plying their trade in the glorified zoo. I've seen it countless times, however, when the uninitiated hunter returns from the field empty-handed. He's angry. Angry at the air taxi operator. Angry at the outcome of his foray. Angry with himself for being duped by the popular media.

One must put Alaska into proper perspective. It's a new land. Geologically, it's not had sufficient time since the last Ice Age to produce a significant layer of nutrient-rich soil. The growing season is short, the winters long. Despite the hype provided by the slick magazines and the touchy-feely Disneyesque films, the carrying capacity of the land for large-bodied animals is small. Minuscule. Microscopic.

Certainly, there are concentration areas where animals are abundant. On the other hand, there are thousands upon thousands of square miles where biomass of big game animals is staggeringly low. The land usually can't support any more than are there.

Inimical factors are many. Most of the big game species are negatively affected by countless hazards during their normal life span. Diseases and parasites are generally few in the harsh northern climate, but certainly can affect some populations. Predators are seemingly always hungry, looking for a meal. Man has recently become a major player in the ecology of population dynamics, bringing with him a wide array of transportation methods and weapons with which to prey on big game animals. Weather factors, especially during the long, harsh winters, are periodically responsible for tremendous mortality. If one looks at reality, much of interior Alaska can be legitimately likened to a biological desert.

In my current situation, the absolute middle of the Sahara would have probably been more congenial. Survival depended on my daily abilities to secure enough food to subsist for that single day. I put out as many squirrel snares each day as the short daylight would allow. Obviously, though, it was touch-and-go on a daily basis concerning whether or not I could manage to input the energy required to continue for another twenty-four-hour period.

Since dropping out of the mountains and down into the margins of the interior taiga, I was thankful for the availability of firewood. However, the lack of food was certainly becoming life-threatening. I became less willing to put forth the effort to sustain my own life. Had I not happened upon the moose tracks in the snow, I doubt if I'd have made it another week before succumbing to the elements.

The tracks appeared to have been made the previous night. A single animal had moved along the lake margin, just as I had been attempting to do. The ten-day-long storm had dictated that I camp and await better traveling conditions, but the travels of the long-legged moose were little affected by the three-foot snows that had accumulated. Thinking that I could perhaps follow the tracks and catch up to the animal renewed my spirit.

I returned to camp and gathered my meager belongings. The storm appeared to be breaking, and I was cognizant of the fact that I needed to drastically change my routine. Either I could die (which wouldn't constitute much of a change), or I could make an attempt to catch up to the moose. How far would he travel before settling down in a patch of willows for the remainder of the winter, or at least for a few days?

I soon realized that travel through the waist-deep snow was impossible. I'd been checking my squirrel snares daily, so was able to maintain those trails close to camp. However, the untrammeled snow was an entirely new, virtually impossible nightmare.

My mind was one-tracked. I needed that moose. This was the first set of fresh tracks I'd seen in more than a month that were made by something larger than a snowshoe hare. How was it going to be possible?

Pulling the makeshift toboggan behind me, I struggled on one good leg and a crutch through the snow for several hours. In only that short time, I was utterly exhausted. Sweat and thawed snow mixed on my skin and clothing to ensure I was completely soaked. It obviously was not going to work.

As I squatted in the trail left by the moose, I admitted defeat. I had nothing left in me. It would be so much easier just to lie down and sleep. Let that blanket of death cover my eyes and envelop my soul. How easy it was going to be.

As I began to doze off lying exposed in the drifting snow, I thought of Gus and of Sarah. *Would they forgive me for throwing in the towel? For quitting?*

IV
REBIRTH

The eerie wailing of the distant wolf pack and the gnawing cold pierced my impassive senses. Was I going to be cheated out of an easy exit from this earthly existence? Uncontrollable shivering brought me out of my dreamy reverie.

I shook my head, sending half-melted snow in all directions. The near-constant howling of what sounded like more than a dozen wolves was hauntingly familiar. They'd interrupted my downward spiral into oblivion. My thoughts began to become more lucid, more from the severe discomfort of the invasive cold than from a conscious desire to survive. I fumbled at the base of a nearby dwarf spruce to break off a handful of dry twigs and needles with which to start a fire. My hands were numb from the cold and refused to function with any semblance of direction. It took three of my precious matches to start a fire.

The wolves continued their long wailing howls intermittently for at least the next two hours while I added larger and larger sticks to the blaze. The clear, cold night air carried the sound well, and it seemed they were no more than a mile distant. I huddled by the fire throughout the night, thawing my frigid body and trying to dry my ratty, tattered clothing.

As morning's first hint of light developed over the eastern ridges, and with a crackling fire to warm my body and soul, I was again determined to survive. Perhaps the wolf pack was at an old kill site, and I could sneak close enough to kill one. I'd never tried eating a wolf, and I couldn't imagine they would be overly tasty, but the prospect of an animal, any animal, eighty or a hundred pounds, was inviting. As I wavered between my defeatist attitude of the previous night and more positive thoughts of surviving, I envisioned a new plan.

Instead of dragging the toboggan behind me, why not sit or even lie down in the thing and paddle myself along? Might not work real well in the deep fluffy stuff, but may be better than gimping along on one leg and a stump.

After consuming the last of the squirrels I'd salvaged from the snares and boiling the small bones for a hot broth, I rearranged the few contents of the sled. I found that by sitting upright, I was able to make some headway by paddling along with my hands or by using my crutch to push myself along. It seemed much more efficient than walking along while pulling the sled behind me.

Travel was still frustratingly slow, but I was making progress along the trail of the moose. Where the trail dipped slightly downhill, I found that by lying down on the toboggan and using gravity to its fullest advantage, I was actually making reasonable headway. The steeper inclines still necessitated getting out and pulling the sled behind.

I'd made probably half or three-quarters of a mile by the time it became too dark to push any further. The wolves howled less often, but unquestionably closer. Noise made during my travel was muffled by the still-fluffy snow. A light breeze opposite my direction of travel carried my scent to the south, away from where the pack was camped.

For the wolves to stay so long in one location, there must be a source of food. Was there a small opening in the now-present lake ice where the wolves were feasting on late-run salmon? Had they killed the moose I'd been following?

Rather than advertising my presence, I decided that I'd have a much better chance of surprising them tomorrow if I could put up with a cold camp for the night. I dug a shallow trench in the snow and bedded the bottom with my toboggan. It was relatively easy to crisscross spruce boughs over the top of the trench and cover them with the folded tent, then insulate the makeshift roof with a two-foot layer of fluffy, dry snow. I was still uncomfortable and cold, but the strenuous rigors of the days' travels ensured that I slept deeply.

Well before dawn's light, I was on the trail once again. I'd made relatively good progress for at least two hours. I drove myself hard, frustrated by the fact that I hadn't heard the wolves all morning. Had they moved on from whatever it was that had captivated their attention for the last two days?

As I glissaded down a short slope through the scattered spruce, a stench invaded my senses like a cannon shell explosion. The smell of wolf was unmistakable. Normally an utterly repulsive, wild smell, it seemed in this instance a pleasant, fragrant aroma. It meant they were still about, and it meant they were close.

I had gone no more than another hundred yards when I emerged from the edge of the trees into a sparsely forested bog. There they were.

The wolves were absolutely motionless, staring toward me with an intensity I'd never experienced. The only telltale sign of life from them was thin tendrils of vapor that rose from their mouths and nostrils, dissipating as it cooled. A smaller black near the steaming carcass of the dead moose finally looked away and yapped. Gradually then, a few others resumed their feeding frenzy, never without a glance in my direction every few seconds. I counted eleven wolves, a mixture of blacks and grays.

As I lay motionless in my toboggan a mere two hundred feet away, two of the wolves approached. They plowed through the chest-deep snow for a few seconds, stopped to stare through me, then continued their advance. Their piercing eyes left me with the impression that they never really looked at me, but rather, their vision seemed to bore through me to focus several yards behind. It was as if they had found nothing of great interest behind my eyes, so they looked for a deeper meaning beyond.

When they had cut the distance in half, they stopped again, intense yellow eyes never wavering.

My own curiosity was piqued. Why hadn't these wolves scattered? Why had they allowed me to interrupt their dining, without showing the slightest trace of fear? Finally, the proverbial light blinked on in my dense skull. They didn't know I was human. The fur pulled tightly around my head. The prone, straight-on aspect. The lack of scent wafting in their direction.

My previous experiences with wolves, and there were many, were almost always very short-lived, usually punctuated with the wolves disappearing in short order. But I'd always provided them with some cue, visual, auditory, or olfactory, of what and where I was. These wolves were obviously not alarmed, having been presented with a curiosity to ponder rather than a threat to their safety. Despite the common belief that wolves attack people, my experiences proved this idea to be completely bogus.

After a period of probably twenty minutes, the large black nearest me sat down, soon to be followed by the gray. He looked back at the feast, slightly raised his chin, and began to howl. He started with a barely audible low, guttural noise, building in volume as his voice climbed the scale. As his first howl was trailing off, others in the pack joined the chorus. At this distance with the cold, dense air, the intensity of the serenade left me awestruck. I had heard individuals and entire packs howling countless times before, but never with this clarity and power. I can easily understand how humans could be emotionally duped by the hordes of environmentalist nature-fakers that had elevated the wolf to a status equal to that of gods of past civilizations.

As galvanizing as the situation was, I still had to maintain a realistic perspective. I needed another blanket, and I needed food. At this point, there was no question in my mind what my action would be, as both food and clothing were available right in front of me. From my position, it took little time to line up the crosshairs on the chest of the largest gray and squeeze the trigger.

At the deafening report of the rifle, there was immediate chaos. Wolves wheeled and departed in all directions away from me. The targeted gray lay twitching a few feet from the still-steaming moose carcass. The other ten had disappeared into the trees.

They left behind ample evidence of their presence. I skidded along in the fluffy snow, hardly noticing the hundreds of saucer-sized wolf prints intermingled with tracks of their fallen prey. Wisps of moose hair and splatters of crimson looked out of place in the pristine snow. As I neared the kill site, great black mounds of wolf shit dotted the trails. Ravens croaked from nearby trees, probably thankful that the wolves had departed, but still unwilling to approach and contend with whatever that strange creature was who had entered the scene.

The carcass had been savagely ripped open by the same powerful jaws that had brought it down. It was a mature bull, evidenced by the overall size and the large chalk-white antler pedicels from which massive antlers must have recently dropped. The nose and ears had been chewed off, whether before or after death I would never know. The rumen, intestines, and other abdominal organs remained, but the ribs protecting the heart, liver, and lungs had been gnawed through at the brisket, and those vitals had been consumed. The skin of the underbelly had been ripped open, almost as if a surgical instrument had facilitated the initial incision. The hide was reflexed back, and the internal fat largely consumed. Moose hair, so well aligned and orderly on the living creature, was now scattered in disarray on the snow, on the brush, and on virtually every square inch of the exposed meat and entrails. It looked as if a stick of dynamite had been used to field dress the animal.

As with every other dead bull moose I'd ever seen, this one was massive. Although I'd killed at least a dozen myself, and had been involved with field dressing, packing, and butchering dozens more, I was always amazed at the enormity of an Alaskan moose. Undoubtedly well over a half a ton, they are the largest hoofed mammal in North America. This was the windfall I'd envisioned in my wildest of dreams. A sweeter and more appropriate gift at this point would be difficult to imagine. The combination of moose meat, wolf blanket, and moose hide for shelter was, in my current situation, absolutely the ultimate gift that could be expected from this usually unforgiving land.

I was able to start a fire, more as a psychological comfort than a physical one. The morning's activities and subsequent excitement had involved more than enough exertion to maintain body heat. Once I'd gathered enough nearby squaw wood to maintain my little blaze for a couple of hours, I began the task of pelting the dead wolf.

As I struggled with the hundred-pound animal, my mind busied itself with memories of earlier times. Times, at least in retrospect, that had been infinitely easier. I remembered Gus and I ambushing five wolves on a caribou kill in the Mulchatna, when we'd pelted all five animals in about an hour and a half. With my current physical infirmities, this job would be at least two hours by itself. Once the hide was off, it would be another several hours, maybe days, before I'd be finished with the fleshing. I took small consolation in knowing that I wouldn't need to prepare this hide for the taxidermist. All I needed was a warm pelt to keep the relentless frost from invading my bones.

I liken dull knives to lawyers; both are virtually as worthless as legs on an egg, except perhaps for spreading butter or bullshit. Fortunately through all my floundering in the snow along with all the other misfortunes, I'd been able to keep my small pocket sharpener from disappearing, and I began the task by honing the main blade on my small folding knife.

Rough skinning the wolf was completed in reasonable time, while maintaining a watch for the inevitable return of the pack. I'd spent enough time in the woods to know that they posed no threat to me, but I was greedy enough to hope for another shot . . . potentially another blanket. Every few minutes I was serenaded by a distant howl, usually joined by a second and third, then what sounded to be the full orchestra of the remaining pack. They sounded as if they had regrouped and were fading away to the north and east, looking for an easier meal elsewhere.

Once I removed the wolf hide, I became aware of a fantastic hunger and thirst that roared up from my gut (I doubt it had much to do with the incredible stench from the bloating, steaming wolf carcass). The fire felt good, and I began stick-roasting small strips of moose rib meat over the fire. Moose meat never tasted so good. My small pot of now-melting snow produced needed liquids, refill after refill.

Life was good. I was noticeably euphoric over my recent good fortune, and for the first time in at least two months, I actually imagined that I had a fighting chance at life.

Even with the fire, the advancing darkness and the plummeting temperatures made it all but impossible to maintain progress in taking care of the moose. It felt good to have a belly full of fresh meat, being the first time in recent memory that I'd truly felt sated. The day had been long, and I'd decided hours before that there was no sense in trying to rush the situation. I had successfully taken over the moose from the wolf pack much the way a spring grizzly will viciously and arrogantly do, and I wasn't about to relinquish my claim.

Through the early part of the evening, I dozed by the fire, my idle thoughts again with Sarah and First Gold Creek. The fresh wolf pelt was already put to use, both as an insulating mat underneath me in the toboggan, as well as wrapped over the top as a blanket. As the night wore on, it was obvious that I was in for a long one. Without a thermometer, it was, of course, impossible to be exact, but I figured the temperature had dropped to somewhere near fifty below by midnight, and even with the new wolf blanket and a full belly, I was hard-pressed to maintain my body heat. As I lay in the sled, my face all but buried in the wolf fur, I could look opposite the small fire and still see steam rising steadily from the now-cooling moose carcass. I'd been able to eviscerate it completely and had propped the chest cavity open to the frigid air. As I contemplated the steaming carcass, an idea came to me. Why not climb into the chest cavity and let the belly skin drape across the ventral opening, using the retained body heat of the huge animal to keep me warm, instead of watching the body heat dissipate into the cold night? Perhaps it would be sufficiently warm to enable me to simply let the fire die down. What the hell!

With little effort, I was able to take advantage of the meat and fur situation a bit further. I found the chest and gut cavity to be a bit cramped and bloody, but the heat retained in the massive animal was immediately obvious. Sleep came fast and deep.

Morning arrived without my usual activity. I remembered waking a time or two, reveling in the fact that I was neither cold nor hungry. Certainly a nice change of pace. My attitude had been remarkably reversed in the short span of less than a day's time. All seemed well with the world. All seemed well, that is, until the gluttonous meal of almost pure protein of the evening before worked its way, with astounding rapidity, through my lower bowels.

I thought, *Simple, huh?* I lift the hide a bit, reflex back the ribs from over top of me, and crawl out.

What I hadn't considered though, was that the meat of the ribs and the encasing overlain hide, having had a full night to cool, was now frozen quite solid. Solid as a rock. Solid as a big rock.

I had not anticipated this turn of events. I was entombed in an inescapable little crypt. Wouldn't the wolves or wolverines be pleasantly surprised when they returned, finding a nice little dessert, however indelectable, awaiting them inside, frozen solid?

After the initial twinge of panic, my first thought was that even frozen tissue could be hacked and sawed through with a knife, and I could exit. Hell, with the smallest opening, even the ravens were capable of accessing meat through the thick hide of a moose.

The pressure from my previous night's meal was uncomfortable by this time, but at least it was partially overpowered by my panicked desire to get out of the coffin. I wiggled my arm down to my pants pocket to retrieve my knife, dislodging condensed ice crystals from the roof of my shelter, and was rewarded with finding absolutely nothing.

With a bit of concerted twisting, I found I could press my greasy, blood-stained, bearded maw against the lower ribs and peek out of the carcass. The fire had died down to near nothingness, leaving a gaping hole in the packed snow. There, stuck upright in the snow, exactly as I had stuck it in the night before, was my pocketknife. It was five or six feet away. May as well have been a mile. How could I be so foolish? Without that knife, I was doomed. In my renewed panic, the confines of the moose's chest cavity seemed to tighten and wouldn't allow me reasonable leverage with either arms or leg. Croaking ravens were still unwilling to come to the "free" meal but remained in nearby trees, apparently understanding the situation. Their croaking and cawing seemed nothing more than a demented desire to poke fun at my predicament.

More wiggling and grunting, and finally I was able to get my arm through the small opening and out into the cold. The exit hole was near the snow level, and with my arm extended out, I was unable to see out of the dark cavern. By feeling around, and then actually into, the fire pit, I was able to grasp a charred end of a spruce stick that hadn't been totally consumed by the fire. I pulled it back into the carcass and, with the stick, was finally able to pry open a larger hole. With considerable effort, even more cussing, and not a minor amount of sweat, I was able to work an opening wide enough to get one arm and my head out of the carcass. I was spurred on by the fact that my bowels refused to remain shut for much longer. I squeezed out of the carcass, dropped my drawers immediately, and relieved the back pressure.

The knife immediately went back into my pocket as I once again vowed to never, never, put it down again. I hollered various obscenities at the ravens; they croaked back, unperturbed.

All's well that ends well, I guess, and I was none the worse for wear following the ordeal. After I'd settled down a bit, refilled my paunch, and began the day's task of removing the now-frozen hide from the moose, I was able to put the episode into perspective. Although I hadn't consciously had reason to do so in months, I had to chuckle to myself. *What a complete dumbshit.* I looked forward to my evening beside the campfire, conjuring all sorts of ways to embellish the fiasco as I entered it into my journal.

My next order of business was to take full advantage of the meat so graciously provided by the wolf pack.

The meat salvage operation was time consuming but, at the same time, entirely satisfying. I could work leisurely at the task without my earlier need to constantly be on the move. I'd been able to resurrect the few remaining embers from the previous nights' blaze to furnish warmth and to sizzle countless strips of meat. Removing the frozen skin of the moose was cold and slow, but with help from the fire, I had the complete right side of the animal skinned before midafternoon darkness settled in. The last duty during the long twilight period was to gather enough wood to keep the small fire alive through the night. Conserving every match was essential, and allowing a fire to completely dwindle to coldness was a mistake I could ill afford.

Ravens refused to leave the stunted spruce perches they had chosen as their vigil posts. Their raucous gossip caught the attention of five or six gray jays, who were a bit less particular than the ravens about their dining company. Unlike their larger black cousins, the jays were immediately amiable, taking full advantage of the benevolence I allowed. Had it been a day or two earlier, their willingness to mingle so close would have been rewarded with a concerted attempt to add them to the stewpot. Now I had a bit more palatable fare, and their squawkings and scoldings at each other were tolerable. One darker-headed youngster, in particular, saw nothing wrong with perching atop my head as I struggled with the carcass of the bull.

A death in the Alaskan winter, especially the death of an animal of this mass, was a blessing to a variety of predators and scavengers. Very little went to waste. The livelihood of nearly all was made a bit easier by the death of one. Wolves generally feasted for a day or two then moved on in search of fresher cuisine, often returning weeks or even months later to crunch and crack the long bones for the energy-rich marrow. Wolverines, foxes, marten, and weasels were then afforded an opportunity for sustenance. Ravens and gray jays, as well as chickadees and magpies, scavenged whatever they could find throughout the "life" of the diminishing carcass. Voles and shrews were nearly always present under the snow, boring up from their subnivean burrows and runways to excavate caves and caverns through the undersides of the carcass. Goshawks, hawk owls, and boreal owls were often lured by the activity, preying upon others that were there for the feast. Many a squirrel or sparrow nest had been lined with the hollow, insulating hair of a winter-killed moose. Porcupines wandered from afar in the spring to chew the remaining bones, hooves, or antlers for minerals and salts or simply to chisel down their ever-growing incisors. Waste did not happen out here.

The third day spent at the kill site afforded an opportunity for further work, as well as enabling an assessment of the situation and formulating future plans. Although the air temperature remained excruciatingly low, I was able to complete the skinning. Instead of one fire to maintain my warmth and help thaw the carcass, I surrounded the fallen moose with three blazes. I commented time after time in my journal notes how fortunate I'd been to find this carcass and find it in a place with adequate firewood close by.

Almost all immediate needs were supplied. Food, although woefully unbalanced, was obviously taken care of. Water too was of course not a problem, what with the combination of snow everywhere, fire, and the small aluminum pot I had. Shelter from the relentless cold had been supplemented by the fact that I now had additional raw materials at my disposal.

Realizing that I'd be unlikely to come across another windfall as grand as this moose, I made the most I could of the opportunity. With spruce poles and snare wire, a frame was constructed for a lean-to. It was backed by the now-unused toboggan and roofed over by the huge moose hide. I banked snow against the back and sides, eliminating drafts from three directions. A large fire pit was maintained in front, reflecting back into the lean-to. Spruce boughs were stacked in layers eight or ten deep on the floor, insulating me from the invasive cold of the frozen snow and ground below.

For the next two weeks, my existence alternated between gathering firewood and butchering and smoke-drying strips of moose meat. While processing the valuable meat into jerky, I soon realized that to do so successfully required constant attention. Not that the temperature or the amount of smoke was critical (or even important), but rather, the fact that the "pet" gray jays were consummate thieves and would quickly steal every tidbit and morsel that wasn't actively defended.

The ravens had evidently decided that there were greener pastures elsewhere, probably following the wolf pack to a new kill site where they could compete with each other and the myriad four-legged beasts rather than competing with me. Daily, however, a single or pair would invariably return, croak their disappointment or displeasure, and continue their travels. It amazed me that they continued their daily flights even in the minus fifty- or sixty-degree cold. What astounding and untold secrets do they harbor in order to contend with the severe arctic conditions? As mankind has done for eons, I was acutely envious of their abilities to fly, as well as their seeming imperviousness to the cold. It is easy to understand and empathize with various early civilizations that revered the raven.

Once the meat was sufficiently dried and the hides fleshed out so they wouldn't rot, I had to once again strike out to the north toward civilization. Breaking camp was difficult, more from the mental aspect than the physical. I had to continue. I had to return to my Sarah.

The snowpack was heavy. Finding anything to supplement my meat diet was becoming increasingly difficult, and my health was noticeably deteriorating. Bleeding gums and several loose teeth, as well as sore muscles and aching joints, were a constant reminder that necessary vitamins and minerals were lacking. Scurvy, I was finding out, was the scourge not only of the ancient mariners, but of wayward sheep hunters as well. The trek down the glacier out of the godforsaken mountains, looking back, had been a time of plenty. At that point, I'd still had some holdover food that Gus and I had brought in. I'd had meat from our first sheep, as well as from the lamb I'd shot. I remember whining and complaining to myself at the time; but I was now well aware that that time was, in comparison to now, a time of relative ease. Will I look back another month from now and reminisce about this being the "good old days"? *Would I be alive to be able to reminisce?*

Now, there were days when I would spend from dawn until dusk searching through the snow on my hands and knees for a handful of cranberries. I had taken one of the moose's shoulder blades and attached it to a short black spruce pole in an attempt to produce a reasonable facsimile of a shovel. Indeed, it did make the snow sweeping much easier, although nowhere did I find berries plentiful.

I raided squirrel middens containing winter caches of cones whenever they were encountered, and I spent countless hours by firelight extracting the minute seeds from the spruce cones. Freeze-dried mushrooms were sometimes found as well, and they continued to be a welcome addition to my meat soup.

Periodically, I encountered a rose hip or two on sturdy stems that had not succumbed to the weight of the winter's accumulation of snow. At such times, I usually took time to dig and brush away snow from the entire bush, looking for additional fruit. These were high in vitamin C and would certainly serve to retard the inevitable onset of scurvy. Three or four rose hips were added to water, usually making four or five weak cups of evening tea, before the seeds and other dregs were chewed and consumed. Again, nothing was wasted.

The days were getting noticeably longer, although temperatures and winds were not significantly different than they'd been over the past two months. The frequency of storms had not diminished, nor had their intensity. I tried to maintain a journal with my odd variety of entries (numbers of berries found, squirrel tracks encountered, temperatures, philosophical musings) but was unable to accurately recount the early period of the trip. I now suspected that mid-January had arrived.

I knew the country relatively well, having hunted in the Nelchina Basin several times. I had been moving north along the east margin of Tazlina Glacier. That miserable piece of ice had terminated at the lake of the same name, and I had continued to move sporadically north along the margin of the lake. I had planned all along to cut across the lake near its northeastern end just upstream of the outlet and continue another twenty miles or so to the north where I would hopefully intersect the Glenn Highway.

I had moved now out away from the mountains and was traveling through a small series of foothills, still more or less following the margins of the lake. It was there that I encountered my next possible meal ticket. Although my stores of frozen or dried meat were better than ever, passing up an additional opportunity would have been nothing but foolish.

Movement. That predatory instinct present in all of us, yet usually hidden beneath multiple layers of humanity, had surfaced in me; and all senses were cued toward survival. Peripheral senses had first detected the movement atop the ice and snow bordering the trees. Finally . . . something bigger than a gray jay and vastly more attainable than a moose was visible as a moving black dot against the tiresome white background a couple hundred yards away.

My first thoughts were of porcupine. Then a few moments of despair when I guessed the distant undefined form was probably a wolverine. I knew enough about them to know they were tremendous wanderers, far more mobile than I, and probably not worth the effort even if I were able to kill one. As I continued to stare across the leaden landscape, rendered so by the thick late afternoon thaw, I realized that my first two thoughts were wrong. It was a beaver. One who obviously was bored with his previous six months of cached, soggy willows and had escaped the iced-in confines of the winter pond to explore the delicacies of fresher fare available topside. Often, I remembered, beavers take advantage of early spring thaws by gnawing or clawing their way through the ice and snow to seek out fresher vegetation, usually only to return to their wintry confines below the ice when winter retakes its icy grip on the country. So long as this animal was out, however, its tasty, rich meat was definitely worth the effort.

The predatory response was exciting. And beaver meat was excellent. Even a medium beaver would provide twenty pounds of life-giving protein. Additionally, it was possible that I could kill this mobile meal even without the use of my firearm.

I watched from my original vantage point as the beaver plowed through the snow, making a rut behind itself as it headed unerringly toward a small stand of birch trees. It was obvious that the beaver could not see out of the rut he was in, but his trail was straight toward the birch. Was he headed toward the food source on memory alone, or was there some faint smell that enabled him to home in on the birches? Whatever it was, it now took him at least twenty yards from his exit hole in the ice.

I formulated a simple plan. It was to let the beaver arrive at the trees, at which time I would place myself alongside the trough, wielding a large club, between the beaver and his hole in the ice. I could then, I assumed, simply whack him on the skull as he passed back along his rut; and I would eat well on something other than moose for a day or two.

As I watched, the beaver maintained his course straight at the birches, picked out a small one near the front, and immediately began his logging operation. I dropped my toboggan tow line and hobbled across the snow toward him. Before I was halfway, however, he had completed his task of felling the twenty-foot tree, and he began nibbling at the tips of the branches. Fortunately, this occupied him for another thirty minutes or so and allowed me to position myself at the ambush site.

No sooner had I arrived than the beaver began dragging the entire tree back down the trail, headed back toward the opening in the ice. My plan seemed to be working perfectly. When the beaver was no more than three yards from me, I jumped up from my hiding spot near his trail and rushed (as well as I could on one leg and a crutch) at him. I hadn't anticipated his response. I'd assumed that he'd probably drop the tree and retreat back up the trail. Quite the opposite actually occurred.

The beaver was aware of me immediately, dropped the butt of the tree he was skidding along behind him, and jumped at me. I was more than surprised at his unanticipated aggression, and I was the one who was taken aback. Because of this "attack," I fell back onto the snow, swinging the club wildly. While I didn't make contact with the beaver, I did make quite solid contact with my one remaining shin. The beaver, with more agility than I thought possible, bounded over my leg and down the trail back to the hole. In seconds, the entire scenario had played out, and I was left with nothing to do but laugh at myself for my naiveté and awkwardness.

I remained at the beaver trail for the rest of the day, assuming that the beaver would reemerge to collect his groceries. Unfortunately, in the next twenty-four hours, he didn't return; and upon examination of the refrozen hole in the ice, it was apparent that the beaver was probably content to wait another couple of months before he exited his dark and watery domain. I was left with only a lesson learned: I would not again be lulled into thinking that I could anticipate the actions of an animal that had had eons of natural selection upon which to rely for his survival.

Sarah and Mattie had continued their close relationship, bound together by their common misfortune and grief. They had returned to their lives in Anchorage, trying to pick up the pieces and put things back together. For both, times were difficult. Financially, both were comfortable. Far more important, however, was the overwhelming need for closure. Accepting the harsh fact that their lives were forever changed by the absence of their respective mates was a daily trial. Both were unwilling to accept the fact that they would probably never again see, talk with, or embrace their respective partners.

For each of them, some days were better than others. The long, dark nights of northern winters, when skies were leaden and heavy with snow, were depressing. As the February days lengthened and periodic days of sunshine highlighted the Chugach Range behind the city, life was a bit more tolerable. In earlier years, Sarah had looked forward to the early spring weather and the chance to spend weekends skiing in the mountains. This year, however, she unconsciously avoided any association with the wilds. It was a painful reminder that somewhere, hidden in the hills, perhaps submerged in hundreds of feet of glacial water, lay her most cherished belonging.

Periodically, though, Sarah would feel the pangs of emptiness subside and an inner calm come over her, as if Charlie were assuring her from afar that everything would turn out all right. Although too practical a person to truly believe in paranormal hocus-pocus, she nonetheless accepted these fleeting hours appreciatively.

Sarah and Mattie rarely broached the subject of the upcoming search for Gus, Charlie, and Mica. They'd agreed with Anna following the disaster last fall that a search of the lake must ensue, but probably not until June when the ice was gone. As with any disaster striking the heart, the need for closure was paramount. Counselors dwelled on the need for the grief-stricken to accept the fact that there was no turning the clock back. To resume any normalcy in their lives, they must get over the grief and accept the facts, as bitter as they may be. Sarah invariably nodded her head in agreement but, thus far, was unable, or unwilling, to accept that Charlie was dead. Perhaps the search of the lake would yield the bodies, and despite the shock associated with such a merciless procedure, there would be finality.

Anna was understandably coping better than Sarah and Mattie. The ordeal had brought her and Tom together, and with Tom spending more and more time at the Meyers' place, the normal chaotic activities of the day precluded dwelling on negative emotions. Anna, of course, missed her father tremendously and periodically was unable to contain her emotions, breaking down in miserable fits of crying and depression. But at least Tom was always around to console her.

Another week of sporadic and labored travel brought me to the lake crossing point. A full day of travel now consisted of only perhaps a half mile of ground covered. Snow was deep and fluffy, and virtually every foot gained was only with the utmost of resolve. Traveling in the sled was impossible due to the snow conditions. I was again forced to tow it behind me. My good leg and opposite armpit were both raw and inflamed at the end of a day's travel. Layover days were occupied by eating, trying to stay warm, and drying the snow- and sweat-soaked clothing from the previous day. Several days had been spent searching out frozen berries or other food. Although I hadn't progressed from the previous campsite on these particular days, I felt that maintaining food input was worth the added time and effort.

Tazlina Lake, at the point I had picked to cross over to the western side, was only about a mile wide. I spent an entire day readying myself and my meager belongings for the journey. In case the crossing was impossible to complete in one day, I included a small bundle of firewood in my sled. From the campsite on the eastern margin, the weather on the morning of my departure seemed no worse than any of the previous four or five days. A moderate breeze blew the length of the lake from the south, and the temperature was somewhere around minus twenty. The sky was thinly overcast, creating halo-like sun dogs in the early southeastern sky.

I departed in the half-light of early dawn. The margin of the lake proved relatively easygoing, although the snow had drifted to more than six feet in some places. During the first hour of the crossing, winds increased noticeably. By midday, I had hoped to be somewhere approaching midway across the lake. However, the incessant wind had created a ground blizzard, and it became nearly impossible to maintain my balance in the white-out conditions. Periodically too, I found I was unable to see either shoreline. The blizzard had not only made it impossible to maintain a straight course, but had become so intense that the sun was obliterated.

Along with my complete inability to navigate, I was now trying to move through several inches of slush beneath the snow. One of the ever-present dangers of travel in the far north is the constant threat of that miserable phenomenon known as overflow. Although not completely predictable, it seems to occur when heavy snows accumulate on lakes and rivers, weighing down the ice. As the pressures increase from the weight, cracks develop in the ice, and water seeps from beneath, upward onto the ice surface. Snow, of course, is a great insulator; and the water, even when air temperatures are excruciatingly low, remains in its liquid form. Traversing lakes or rivers that have overflow beneath the blanket of snow has caused immeasurable inconveniences to northern trappers and travelers since the dawn of time. Countless deaths can certainly be blamed on it.

The inability to navigate and the difficulties of slogging through the overflow left me with no options. The storm produced swirling winds that couldn't be counted on to provide any indication of a constant direction. The leaden sky provided no clue of the direction of the sun. To avoid wandering aimlessly on the snow-covered ice, I decided to make a camp for the remainder of the afternoon. I hoped that, as evening approached, the winds would diminish; and I could again navigate using the shoreline or the stars.

I packed down a trench in the snow roughly two by six feet, building up the bottom with surrounding snow to keep the floor from becoming wet with the overflow. Once I had that completed, the frigid temperature quickly hardened the indentation, making it as hard as concrete. I bundled myself in the moose hide robe and wolf pelt and tilted the toboggan over top of me, awaiting an end to the raging storm. Rather than trying to start, then maintain, a campfire, I decided to save the meager bundle of sticks until the wind abated.

Although I was well insulated from the tempest that blew all around me, I could detect no prolonged differences in the sound of the wind for several hours. Darkness enveloped me in very little time. I was aware of the fact that not only was the weak wintertime sun dropping unseen below the southwestern horizon, but the blowing snow was quickly covering me as well, accelerating the onset of darkness.

I slept periodically and fitfully throughout the night. Wind sifted the fine snow into every crack and crevice, packing it tightly around my makeshift cocoon. Fortunately, the untanned moose hide was stiff enough to provide a casing around me that didn't conform to my various postures, and I could alternate prone positions without undue effort or contortions. The moose hide, wolf fur, and blanket of wind-driven snow combined to provide a well-insulated, although tiny, shelter. Even without a fire, my body heat was contained well enough to provide a comfortable sleeping environment.

Without a clue as to the time of day, disoriented from the absolute lack of light and barely able to move in my cramped, claustrophobic quarters, I struggled awake in a panic. Had the same moose hide become a tomb for me once more? It seemed that the hide had become a bit more supple with the constant use it had received over the previous five or six weeks. The encasement that I was confined within was probably more due to the wind-packed snow than to the hide itself, and once I realized that, the panic subsided. I was able, finally, to open the hide enough to begin digging up through the snow; and the light filtering through made the duty bearable. Within ten minutes, I had burrowed my arm up through the snow and was able to construct a chimney through which fresh air could circulate. It took probably another twenty or thirty minutes to scrape away enough snow to emerge from the night's den. When I was finally able to poke my head out of the drift that had formed around my siwash, I experienced mixed emotions. My immediate feelings included a twinge of disappointment, overpowered by elation, followed by simply rolling my eyes, shrugging my shoulders, and accepting the fact that I'd probably made the right decision in the furious storm of the previous afternoon and night. In the daylight and calm following the storm, the north shore of the lake, my prestorm objective of yesterday, was less than a hundred yards distant. I'd survived again, but oh, how much nicer it would have been with some trees for cover and at least the possibility of a soul-warming fire.

I'd learned a lot about myself in the past few months. The ability to maintain health under unbelievably adverse conditions was a marvel. Six months ago, I could have scarcely imagined being put into my current situation and surviving. Now each day of my odyssey was taken in stride, and I felt healthier and stronger by the day. My meager rations, enduring the worst of the elements that the North American continent could throw at me, and adapting to the daily rigors of travel and survival with a major deformity, were all cause for an inner peace. A feeling of accomplishment. Returning to my daily routine in Anchorage would undoubtedly be accepted but would perhaps lack real purpose. In some ways now, it seemed empty.

The weather, always variable during the early spring of the year, had indeed changed dramatically from the blizzard of yesterday. The dull gray calm following a severe storm had settled into the basin, and the air was absolutely still. Had there been any snowflakes, their descent from whatever altitude would have been a direct, slow fall, influenced by gravity alone. The passing front that was yesterday's nightmare was followed by warming temperatures, probably well above zero on this midmorning March day.

Despite my urge to travel once again, I needed another day at the north margin of the lake to eat and attend to various duties. An abundance of good wood was available, and after the day's duties were complete, I was able to start another fire. *How many campfires had I made over the past months? How many future hunters, trappers, miners, or explorers would find my leftover charcoal and wonder to themselves who had passed before them?*

With my back to the small night fire, I mused at the sporadic orange glow bouncing off nearby spruce, nearly overwhelmed by the brilliance of the full moon. Moonlight twinkled from a million pinpoints of reflection. Each crystal of frozen water winked its brilliance as I, almost imperceptibly, moved my head back and forth. The carpet of white farther in the distance reflected the moonlight with such amazing clarity that details were obvious.

Tracks of a lone ptarmigan a hundred feet distant meandered through the occasional willow tips protruding through the snow. It the full light of day, the tracks would probably have remained unnoticed, but now my dilated pupils drank in the obscure details. The simple splendor was at once soothing and intoxicating. The absolute stillness of the night was broken only by an occasional twig snapping or hissing on the fire.

As dedicated as I was to reaching civilization, I once again questioned my motives. Of course it was paramount that I do everything in my power to "escape" this wilderness. At the same time, would I come to question my own sanity once I was back to what I had heretofore considered reality? With reasonable health restored, would I long for a return to unpeopled places; or would I shun them, afraid of the possibilities?

Despite my best intentions to move on, the next four days were spent on the lake margin. A large beaver lodge was still eight or ten feet above the ice and snow, and the vent hole in the top breathed steam from the lodge members inside. I knew that if I could dig through the snow and debris atop the lodge, the beavers residing within could be harvested for meat. By shoveling with my hands, the top of the lodge was easily uncovered, and the semisweet smell of beaver castor emanated from the numerous small vents. Unfortunately, however, I found that the summer mud and sticks used in the construction were tightly welded together, frozen into an impenetrable cement to ward off marauding bears and wolverines.

I'd heard of Interior Athabaskans in years past that had successfully obtained needed meat, lard, and fur from beavers by hacking and chiseling into lodges. Reputedly, once a hole was established, the resident beavers, of course, would vacate the lodge. However, beneath the winters' ice, they had no place to go to obtain air; and they would invariably return to the "safety" of their lodge, where they could be snatched by waiting hands. I put two days of effort into breaking through the top of the lodge, banking on the stories as being true. The cement of the packed mud was easily thawed when I built a blazing fire on it, and digging was speeded tremendously. I was finally able to make a hole atop the lodge; and sure enough, the beavers periodically came back to the now-cooling interior of the lodge to rest, sleep, breathe, and even preen themselves. Unless I made an inordinate amount of noise or other disturbance trying to enlarge the hole, they seemed unconcerned about their lodge being destroyed above them. From the rope I'd been using to haul my toboggan, I fashioned a lasso to snare first one, then another beaver. Pulling them up out of the hole was another story.

Once I had the rope firmly around their necks, I found I could bring them up to the entrance hole I had made. Their tenacity, however, was beyond my own strength; and I was unable to drag them completely out of the lodge. Finally, out of frustration at having a meat supply so very close, yet still unattainable, I managed to bring the first out of the hole far enough to expose his head. Then, by tying off the rope to a stick half protruding from the mud of the lodge, I could bludgeon the beaver enough to stun him and drag him out of the hole completely. A few more hard blows to the head, and I had forty pounds of fresh, rich meat.

As with most lodges, this one contained a family unit. Two large animals, probably in excess of fifty pounds each, along with three smaller members, were captured and added to the larder. In previous outings over the years where my main objective was to snare beaver for their luxurious fur, I had developed a habit of taking only two beavers out of any particular lodge. With the hole in the top of the lodge exposing the watery exit tunnels to the cold outside air, however, and my overwhelming need to obtain meat for sustenance, I made the relatively easy decision to take the entire colony. I justified this action knowing that had I left some of the members alive, their fate would be sealed when the tunnels froze solid and they no longer had access to their feed caches. Rather than subjecting them to a slow death by starvation or freezing to death, I opted to take the entire group. It was them or me.

Another two days were spent eating the fat-rich meat and drying the leftover shreds for later use on the trail. Like my use of the squirrels, very little was discarded. I now had a dependence on the land that transcended sport or recreational harvesting of resources. The hearts, livers, and kidneys were consumed, as was all the meat, fat, and gristle of the feet and tails. Even the meat of the skulls was boiled and nibbled. Again, the ravens and gray jays were left with very little to scavenge.

V
FINAL PUSH

On the fifth day following my arrival on the north shore, I was again on the move. I knew the Glenn Highway was only fifteen or twenty miles further north, and with reasonable traveling conditions, I could make that distance in less than two weeks' time.

In the spring taiga, however, the traveling was worse than miserable. The previous storm had laid down another foot of snow, and the slight uphill lay of the land made progress all but impossible. The first day of travel yielded a trench about two hundred yards long. At that rate, it would take most of a year to attain the road. Dejected, I returned in less than an hour to the lake margin.

I considered my options. *Should I maintain my northward journey, hoping that the snow conditions would improve? Should I try to take advantage of the lighter snowfall accumulated along the river, heading generally eastward? Perhaps the traveling would be better near the foothills of the Chugach Range. It would be a longer trip in terms of miles, but perhaps shorter in terms of time. Time was of the essence.*

I explored a half mile or so downstream the following day. The traveling was much easier following the river, although the course was meandering, and it might be thirty or forty miles to the road connecting Glennallen and Valdez. Because it was obvious that striking out to the north across country was virtually impossible, I decided to depart to the east, following the river where travel was possible. The canyon through which the river flowed would be out of the wind, and I could perhaps run across moose or caribou along the way. I wasn't sure of the rapids or narrows on the river, but with the severe cold of the winters, I assumed that it would remain frozen, even if there were rapids and falls along the way.

Another day had passed, and I was finally on my way. Traveling along the frozen river was progressing well, although more often than I would have liked, the snow and ice groaned and cracked in noisy protest at my passing. During the first three days of the river travel, I had probably covered nearly two miles and was more than satisfied with my decision to stay along the river. On the fourth day of travel, I was a bit disconcerted to learn that the river had become pinched between bluffs on either side, and the sound of water gurgling and rushing underfoot was louder than I was comfortable with.

Things seemed to be going in my favor for a change. I had reasonable amounts of dried beaver for sustenance and even a few morsels of dried, smoked moose meat. The weather remained stable, with temperatures hovering around twenty below in the early mornings, rising to probably ten or fifteen above by midafternoon. The coming spring was evident from the relative abundance of songbirds. Redpolls and chickadees were constantly chattering, ravens were busy carrying small sticks and whatever other debris they could add to their nests, and snow buntings and Lapland longspurs were moving through in increasing numbers. Great horned and boreal owls hooted and called endlessly throughout the calm nights. Even my assumption that the river corridor might offer meat was apparently correct. I had yet to see a moose, but tracks along the riverbanks were constant.

I came across an old wolf kill, a yearling bull moose, which was probably killed more than a month previously. The ravens and gray jays begrudgingly relinquished their claim, and I was able to find three leg bones that had yet to be cracked open for the marrow. I relished the waxy white marrow that I obtained from these bones, making a broth that was more than worth the effort of breaking open the bones. It provided a hearty meal that would prolong my meager supply of dried beaver meat for yet another day.

Johnny Galbraith had a pretty good trapping year. Fur was abundant, but prices were miserable. Because of this, he had maintained shorter lines than normal; and by mid-February, he had closed and hung his traps. With the season's catch stretched and dried, he had hooked up his small dog team and headed north to the highway, where he would get in touch with Anna or Tom; and they'd get him into town. He was a skillful fur handler, and even with poor pelt prices, he never had any trouble selling his well-prepared pelts to the fur buyer in Glennallen. Once the season's catch was sold, he'd convert his hard-earned cash into staples and return to his little cabin on the lake.

Following his return, it was simply a waiting game for spring to melt the snow and dissipate the ice. Beaver season lasted well into the spring, and he sometimes harvested a couple for new mitts or a hat. One particularly nice spring day following three days stuck in the cabin by a nasty spring blizzard, Johnny decided to head to the east and check out a couple of beaver lodges down near the outlet of the lake. The first of the bank lodges appeared to have a large cache frozen into the ice in front of it and ought to be worth a beaver or two if he took the time to chisel through the four feet of ice to reach the water. While still several hundred yards from the second lodge, however, it was apparent that something was amiss. From a distance, the top of the lodge appeared to have been exploded by a bomb that had sent frozen mud and debris flying in all directions. The otherwise pristine white landscape was scarred with the black mud and broken lodge sticks. Johnny first assumed that a bear had emerged early and had torn into the lodge, but on closer inspection, he was certain it was not the work of a bear. It was apparent that the activities were human. No other animal would have thawed the frozen ground by building a fire.

Johnny was justifiably angry. There were old tracks in the snow where someone had come across the lake to the lodge. Why hadn't they just chipped a hole in the ice near the base of the lodge and set snares? The tracks were covered and largely obscured by new snow and repeated daytime thaws, but judging from the width of the barely discernable path, they must have been riding a snow machine. When he looked into the crater atop the lodge, his anger and disgust heightened. Why would someone be trapping the beaver lodges along his traditional line? Why would they go through the effort of chopping and hacking into the lodge from the top, when beavers were so easy to snare through a hole in the ice? Most of all, why would someone intentionally wipe out an entire colony, either by taking them all or by allowing the lodge to freeze up, denying the remaining beavers access to and from the water? Must be them goddamned city folks from Anchorage that have no respect for the wild animals or the bush way of life.

Three more days brought good traveling. With the end of my ordeal in sight, I found that I'd been putting a bit too much effort into my travels. On the fourth consecutive travel day, I was worn out to the point of utter exhaustion. My armpit was inflamed and painful. My stump of a leg was swollen and beginning to leak again. My supply of beaver meat had been consumed, and hunger had overpowered more intriguing thoughts of Sarah and of putting my life back together. Again, I needed to put all my conscious thought into survival.

I'd become used to the constant sound of running water under my feet, and a bit too complacent about the integrity of the river ice. Because of my exhaustion and lack of food, I'd made a decent camp in a stand of bare willows along the river. On the second day of rest and recuperation, I'd ventured a few hundred yards from the camp in the direction of another visible beaver lodge across the river in hopes of repeating my lodge raiding of a couple of weeks before. As I approached the bank den, the sound of gurgling water was noticeably louder, but I paid little attention. As I neared the lodge, I remember no warning before the ice gave way, and I was plunged into the river. The shock of the excruciatingly cold water brought me fully aware of the predicament I had put myself into.

As my leg and crutch broke through the ice layer, thin because of the constant beaver activity to and from their cache, I fell forward. That ice too was not thick enough to support my weight, but it did break the fall enough that I didn't submerge completely. I thrashed about in the hole, fighting to keep my head above the water line, fighting to keep from being swept beneath the ice by the current, and, at the same time, clawing with my bare and now-bloody fingers at the surrounding shelf of ice. After what seemed like hours in the water, in reality probably no more than a couple of minutes, I was able to pull myself onto ice that would hold my weight. The adrenaline that had fueled my frantic escape now acted to warm my numbed body as I lay motionless on the snow-covered ice shelf.

Minutes passed before the shivering started. I pulled myself further away from the hole, probably eight or ten feet, before I was sure I was in a place the ice would support my weight. I stood and immediately fell back down. In my exhaustion and numbness, my leg was unable to bear any weight. I knew my only hope of surviving yet another disaster would be to return to my camp, where my wolf robe, moose hide blanket, and still-smoldering fire would raise my body's core temperature to near normal.

In the fall through the ice and the frantic aftermath, however, I had dropped my crutch; and it had been swept beneath the remaining ice where it was certainly not retrievable. I sat and rubbed my leg with snow, trying to dry the water and ice, as well as to get the circulation back. I was aware of the bloody snow I was rubbing on my clothes and saw with horror that all my fingers were oozing blood from the frenzied scraping on knife-sharp ice as I tried to extract myself from the freezing water. I felt no pain, however, and I knew that making it back to my camp was now a life-or-death situation. I tried once again to stand; and finding that impossible, I skirted the open water on my hands and knee, crawling as fast as I could through the snow back across the river toward camp. I was endlessly impatient with my progression during my "normal" travels, but the snail's pace on hands and one knee in snow was maddening. I maintained my anger, using it unconsciously to fuel the desire to get back to my camp alive.

Finally, as darkness descended into the canyon, I reached my still-smoldering fire. Thankfully, I had thought to put additional wood nearby. The fire was built up, and as I began to thaw out, an irresistible urge to sleep swept me like an ocean wave, and I succumbed immediately.

I awoke ravenously hungry sometime later. It was dark, and I could feel the clammy dampness of my clothes. That was a good sign. On the flip side of the coin, my fingers were ten sources of acute pain. Upon examination of each individual digit, the cuts, scrapes, and bruises appeared largely superficial; and I assumed that I could handle the pain. In a week or so, they'd be back to normal, with the addition of a few more minor scars.

I made a broth using the last of my beaver meat scraps. I was thankful for the meal but was far from satisfied with the portion. Tomorrow, come stormy weather or a herd of bears, I desperately had to find food.

Little did I know that at this point, I was probably less than two miles from the Glenn Highway. Along this stretch of the Tazlina River, the Glenn Highway parallels it for several miles, generally less than a couple of miles to the north. Being confined to the canyon, however, I was unable to hear the sporadic traffic that barrels along the road. Had I been more familiar with the country, my ordeal may have ended much sooner.

Other circumstances were piled against me also. Little did I realize that this stretch of the river, during most years, had an active trapper working the area for fur. International fur prices had recently dropped to the point that fur trapping was becoming less and less lucrative. This decline in prices led to a concurrent decline in effort on the part of local trappers; thus, this line remained untouched during this particular year. Many people who formerly actively trapped during the winter to supplement their incomes found that their costs exceeded their returns, and they were unwilling to work through the cold and dark of winter for only a few dollars. Trapping was becoming more of a recreational pursuit, with short lines designed to catch enough fur for replacing a worn hat or a pair of mitts or to gather a few pelts to sell to tourists. The availability of government and corporation welfare checks made life in bush Alaska easier, and most people were content to sit at home watching free television and making their way to the post office on a monthly basis to gather their food stamps. True subsistence lifestyles were becoming a thing of the past, a sad commentary on the so-called "independent spirit" of many an Alaskan.

I awoke with a start. The warm spring sun was full in my face, although the air temperature was probably only slightly above zero. I lay there, wrapped in my makeshift blankets, my face a scant inch or two from the snow. Perhaps it stemmed from an inner peace knowing that I had just survived another potential disaster, but I somehow felt warm and secure. I lay in the late-morning sun, confident I could survive any calamity thrown at me. The nighttime freezing temperatures, followed by the thawing afternoon sun, had combined to create an amazing landscape. Dark green spires of spruce were dead calm against the deep blue sky. Closer, near the riverbank, balsam poplar and willow were still bare of leaves but hinted at the coming spring with a lighter shade of green in their branches and boles. Still closer, I marveled at the micro landscape. From a distance of several yards, the impossible white of the glistening snow was water-pool flat. Focusing closer, no more than a few inches from my face, however, the elements had acted in concert to form intricate, perfect swirls. Valleys and ridges, no more than a half-inch tall, were spaced at regular intervals, one side gently rising to the ridgeline, the other side precipitously dropping back to the base, only to begin the next incline. I imagined miniature camels, strung in a line, crossing these dunes in search of the next oasis. In my mind, that oasis was not a grove of date palms surrounding a water hole, but the blackened hole of my campfire, wisps of smoke still rising from the unseen depths.

I forced myself from the reverie, knowing the first order of business upon waking was to maintain the fire. After doing this, I fashioned a makeshift cane from a piece of firewood then set out from camp to find a more reasonable replacement crutch for the one lost yesterday. I rejected several possibilities before finding a gnarled willow that I thought could be worked into a usable crutch, and I returned to camp. During the next several hours, I whittled and hacked and was pleased with the new leg I'd fashioned.

Snares for squirrels were set in two likely places, and I was ecstatic to run across a willow thicket that harbored tracks of snowshoe hares. It was there that I used most of my snare wires in an attempt to catch a bit larger fare for tomorrow's campfire. Following my return to the camp, I was exhausted from the day's rigors and the lack of food and fitfully slept the night sitting upright by the fire, shrouded in wolf fur and moose hide.

At this point in my travels, I knew I had weathered the worst of the winter. Days were progressively longer, and the weather had definitely mellowed. It was springtime. I had feelings of accomplishment, despite the ordeal. I envisioned myself, haggard and filthy from six months of decay, triumphantly pulling myself and my toboggan onto the road, standing triumphantly (on one leg) as I waved down the first passing truck.

I would apologize for my wild looks and even more wild smell, and ask for a lift to the nearest telephone. I'd probably babble on about my travels and adventures. Probably ask for a piece of gum . . . no, chocolate . . . or a cup of coffee. I'd call Sarah first and simply, to the point, ask her to marry me. What had she done in the last six months? She wouldn't think of putting me at the back of her mind. No. We were too much alike for her to lose her faith in my returning to her. She would probably still be chartering planes to look for Gus and me. *What the hell had happened to Mica? What had become of the world I was familiar with?* Too many unanswered questions.

On my seemingly endless trek, putting crutch in front of foot a thousand times a day, I had perhaps too much time now to think and plan for the future. I'd made a solemn promise to Gus that I would do what I could for Mattie. I'd promised to take care of his dog, make sure the animal was treated right, got some bird hunting. I had the answers for a pile of unanswered questions about our plight and about my trip through the wilds of Alaska. Certain people would be anxious to bring out Gus's remains and give him a "proper" burial. I would stand my ground and not let that happen. Gus would be happier lying right where I left him. He was already a part of the wilderness that caused his early departure from this life. I hoped there was something out there after death, something Gus could do to keep occupied with the things he'd always enjoyed.

After the obligatory talks and interviews with various doctors, police, probably a psychologist or two, and a low-life attorney or two (or three, or ten), I'd need to try to reconstruct my life. I'd need to find some way to repay Sarah for all the grief I'd caused her for the past half a year. I realized I was in love with the woman; and despite the fact I'd not seen her for at least six months, I could still vividly imagine her smile, her eyes, her smell. Would she remember me with the same longing?

I was rudely jolted from my reverie by a thunderous crash and continuing rumble. Downriver from my camp no more than three hundred yards, the spring sun had melted the south-facing snows, making it heavy with moisture. The bare slope was unable to hold the weight, and the avalanche roared down toward the river. From my vantage point, there was little danger, but had I been foolish or unlucky enough to camp in the avalanche's path, I'd have been hurled through the melee like a rag doll. As it was, I watched in awe as the tremendous weight of the wave of snow sheared off bottom-lying trees and shrubs, before coming to a tenuous halt on the frozen river. Clouds of snow hung in the air. A thunderous roar crashed off the opposite cliffs, echoing down the gorge. Knowing the newly formed snow barrier would probably be a bit unstable for the next several hours, I was content to count my blessings and remain in my camp. I would continue my journey in a day or two when the alternating night's chill and daytime thaws had set up the avalanche chute, making it a bit more inviting for travel.

The following day, the snares held two rabbits, one entire, the other obviously scavenged sometime during the night by a great-horned or great gray owl. Nonetheless, I was pleased with my success. The salvaged parts were broiled on a green willow over the fire, and I ravenously consumed the entire catch. The skins were used to wrap the top of my new crutch as a pad for my armpit. I gathered the snares that I'd set yesterday for squirrels and repositioned them in the rabbit trails in hopes of a larger catch tomorrow.

Sign of life was more obvious here than anywhere along my previous journey. Perhaps the elevation difference or the varied topography was more inviting for a variety of animals, as tracks were plentiful. I came across a set of porcupine tracks crossing my snare trail, and after only about an hour, I had tracked the animal to a large spruce tree. I could see the quill pig in the tree but was at a loss at how to get it. Finally, I climbed the tree that the porky was in and again was able to bludgeon the seemingly dull-witted animal, knocking it out of the tree after several poorly aimed blows. When I finally climbed down out of the tree, I found that the hapless critter was not yet dead and had to track his bloody trail another hundred yards or so, before issuing the *coup de grace*. Like the rabbits, I consumed the porcupine in its entirety, discarding only the marrowless larger bones, and in this case, the hide and quills.

Although eager to continue on to the east toward civilization, I camped at the spot for another two days. I remained successful at capturing rabbits and, in addition to the four I consumed, had five additional carcasses frozen for the days ahead.

The next two weeks brought little change. I had enough meat to maintain my strength during the travels and came across another wolf-killed moose. I was able to scavenge a couple of meals worth of meat from the moose's neck and head, as well as the marrow I extracted from a few of the long bones strewn about the kill site. I passed more and more open water, but after my earlier incident near the beaver lodge, I was a bit more careful in areas I suspected had thin ice. Spring was advancing, and most afternoons were sunny and pleasantly warm. Water dripped from exposed dark surfaces, and south-facing slopes above the river were becoming bare. When snow-free hillsides were close to the river, I'd divert my route through them, finding a few lowbush cranberries and crowberries to nibble or add to my fire-warmed water. I knew that any day I would finally arrive at the Tazlina River bridge, finally free from the grip of my wilderness winter.

I dreamed one night of hearing a car horn. I lay awake after the dream, imagining that in the still night air, I could really hear trucks passing over the bridge. But . . . there it was again! The sound was unmistakable. I sat up in my fireside cocoon then stood in the pale spring moonlight, straining my ears for some sign of civilization. All I'd wanted up until six months ago was to leave the sounds, sights, and smells of civilization behind and go to places where I wouldn't be subjected to their invasions. Now, here I was longing, straining my ears, for another confirmation that human beings still existed. *Would I be able to cope with the nightmare of the past half a year? Would Sarah still be there?*

I finally went back to sleep, assuming that what I'd heard was a migrating flock of trumpeter swans, honking their honks, wind rushing through their primaries.

Nevertheless, I awoke early with the hope that I was nearing the end. I set out early, pushing myself harder than normal. I had to be getting close. From memory, I thought that the outlet of Tazlina Lake was only about twenty miles above its confluence with the Copper River, and the bridge was only a half a mile or less above the confluence. I had to have traveled nearly that far by now. Despite the troubles, I'd made at least a mile a day when I traveled.

From quickly reviewing my journal, I'd traveled more than twenty days since the lake. I just had to be near the end.

Late in the afternoon, I made camp for the night. I had pushed too hard, and my body was suffering the consequences. The new crutch was uncomfortable, but the softening snow in the afternoons had to be walked through. I found that early in the mornings, I could propel myself along in the toboggan over the crusty snow, but by about noon, the warmth of the day weakened the crust, and walking, or hobbling, was easier. Most of my travels were done in the early morning, as toboggan use seemed much more efficient. Because of my raw and still-sore fingertips, I'd made a set of short ski poles to push myself along with as I sat upright in the sled.

The wind had come up a bit, drowning out any possibility of hearing the traffic along the road. I dejectedly sat at my campfire, disappointed that I'd not reached my destination on that day. As the sky darkened and the northern lights began to dance, the wind died to a whisper. I moved from the crackling and hissing of the small fire, concentrating on hearing those foreign sounds. Yes! Yes! This was not migrating geese or swans, nor was it the mournful howling of wolves. This was traffic humming by on the road. I could even discern different pitches from different cars. A large truck could be heard gearing down for the climb up the hill after crossing the bridge. The bridge had to be just around the corner, just out of sight! Yes!

I was unable to contain my emotions. I jumped to my one leg. Screamed. Howled at the northern lights. I was as good as home, triumphant in my exodus from the wilderness. I was ecstatic. Against all odds, I had won.

I recklessly set off down the river. The pale moon and the northern lights provided enough light to see my way. I had abandoned my toboggan and its few contents. Wrapped in my forlornly ragged clothes and the wolf hide, I stumbled downriver. Rounding the bend a scant two hundred yards below my campsite, I was stunned to see blazes of light piercing through the darkness. It was no illusion. Those were headlights from cars. I had truly made it. Unable to stifle my cries, unwilling to put off my reunion with mankind, I hopped on down the river. I was less than a quarter mile from the road. Hopping along on determination and excitement, I pushed faster and faster. I wondered to myself how many rings it would take Sarah to answer the phone. How long would it take her to drive to me? How long would we embrace and kiss and cry?

With no more than two hundred yards to go, it happened. I was soaked through from a combination of sweat and melting snow. I had fallen countless times, floundering in the snow. The ice gave no discernable indication that it was weak. Before I could react, I was through it, the current unrelenting, sucking me under the ice. I held on to the shelf but was unable to extricate myself from the pull of the relentless current. I watched the headlights of another car race down the hill and cross the bridge. The undulating curtains of the aurora seemed unusually bright overhead.

Had I been fooling myself all along, thinking I could win a war against the wilds of Alaska? As my frozen, unfeeling fingers refused to maintain purchase on the icy ledge any longer, I slipped slowly, unnoticed by anyone, anything, into the gentle, watery depths of another facet of the wilderness. This wilderness had teased and tortured me for countless miles, countless days. I'd been arrogant enough the think that I could win the battle. I came pretty damned close . . .

EPILOGUE

The lower Tazlina River had kings running this time of year. The two boys scrambled down the embankment, laughing and telling dirty jokes to each other, hardly able to contain their enthusiasm. They carried fishing poles, and their quest was obvious. Growing up on the banks of this and other rivers in the area, they knew how to catch fish. It was a bit early for the good salmon runs to start, but they thought a mid-June Saturday morning was a reasonable time to wet a line and see if they could hook a king.

Their first two hours were fun, but didn't result in any fish for the dinner table. Nick was the older and was a bit more determined than his brother Dale. Bored from the lack of action, and tired of being beat by his older brother in their burping contest, Dale wandered back off the river for twenty yards or so into a grove of spruce. A grouse exploded from beneath the trees in front of him, and he explored a bit to see if he could find the nest. No nest, but he did run across a neat sled. There was moose hair strewn around, and he was cautious about there being a grizzly nearby. He returned to the river and talked Nick into going with him to look over the sled a bit more.

They found an old campfire, a dented pot, and a few other worthless items strewn about. Turning the sled upright, they were rewarded with finding a rusty rifle. They argued heatedly over the rifle. Nick was the best arguer as he was able to use cuss words. Dale knew all the words all right but was still uncomfortable with their use, even around his brother. Dale knew that the rifle was rightfully his because he discovered the sled in the first place. Nick laid claim to the gun, arguing that without him, Dale was scared of the big bad bears and wouldn't have found the rifle anyway. Although not too interesting for either of them, Dale picked up a tattered and soggy notebook. He could barely read the shaky and tiny handwritten entries, but unable to wrest the gun from his bigger brother, he settled with the notebook for the time being. He'd get home first and tell his pa about the gun and was sure he'd have the strongest claim to it.

There were undecipherable entries in the notebook, especially in the beginning. Most of it, however, was readable. Ma and Pa were amazed at the writing and would sit around the dinner table reading particular passages to the two boys and their sister. They wondered from time to time about the name that appeared countless times throughout the notes. Who was this Sarah? They marveled at the vivid imagination of the novelist who had penned the notes and wondered why the notes had been abandoned along the banks of the Tazlina River. Perhaps someday, if they hung on to the notes, someone would take an interest . . .

CPSIA information can be obtained
at www.ICGtesting.com
Printed in the USA
LVOW08s0717230417
531853LV00001B/14/P